THE INDENTURED MAN

The story of William Gaze
Australian Pioneer Settler

by

STEPHEN WARD

Dear Happy Reading
Stephen Ward. (Dad!)
January 2013

*This is an historical novel and all characters and
events depicted in this novel, other than those in the
public domain, are fictitious and any resemblance
to real persons or events is purely coincidental*

For my long suffering wife, Linda, who has lived with the ghosts of my ancestors for many years

WILLIAM GAZE

their eldest son

killed by the natives

on Swan River Island

June 17th 1832

Inscription on the Gaze family memorial stone
St Bartholomew's Church
Churchdown Gloucester

PROLOGUE

April 2012

On the balcony of a café overlooking the Plaza de Armas in Cusco two men sat drinking coffee; they neither knew each other nor had ever met before. One of life's strange coincidences of time and place had thrown them together on that day. It was a hot Easter Sunday morning and the two had found themselves standing near to each other in the crush of local people watching one of those quasi religious-military parades that can only happen in South America. They nodded, acknowledging each other as obvious Europeans across a sea of Peruvian faces. As the final military band goose stepped its way past the Cathedral the crowd began to disperse and made for nearby benches. Sitting, one of the men stood and offered his seat to an elderly Peruvian woman.

"Doing your bit for international relations?" the other man laughed.

" Yeh, God, it's hot! Too hot to be standing out here."

"Right. Here want some water?" A bottle was offered.

"Thanks. Been here long?"

"Just over a week in all but I've just come back off the Inca Trail. You?"

1

"I'm here as a tour guide. I'm taking a group around South America for a few weeks."

"You don't look like the typical tour guide."

"I'm not. I'm an archaeologist but I was asked to step in to guide the group as I know the region fairly well. Where are you from?"

"England"

"Thought I picked up the accent."

"And I would say you're Australian from yours?"

"Right. Bill's the name" and in an incongruous action they formally shook hands. "Got time for a coffee?"

"Steve. All the time in the world as I'm on holiday".

"Look, there's a decent café I know across the square if you like."

And so that is how these two men came to be drinking coffee together in a country far from their respective homes. One an Australian archaeologist, the other a retired English school teacher; connected to each other by a strange coincidental bond of history that they were yet to discover.

CHAPTER 1

October 1828

It was the kind of October morning that made you feel good to be alive. Smoke from cottage chimneys hung lazily in the still air as the village of Churchdown stirred from rural slumber. Dogs stretched and yawned in the early sun and pigs grunted their morning welcome. A cockerel strutted along the lane and stared insolently at the man. William Gaze pulled his jacket closer to his body. It was still early and although the autumn sun still had some warmth the crisp air gave hint of winter frosts to come. He swung the bag of carpenter's tools over his shoulder as he set off at a brisk morning pace past the Green and on through the village, rising steadily upwards over Chosen Hill on his way to the Hiring Fair in Brockworth.

His keen grey eyes took in every detail of the village that he had grown up in. He was twenty eight years old and still single, much to his parents' regret. Not that he hadn't had the chance. There had been Sarah Evans, the Blacksmith's daughter. She was as lovely as a summer morning and he had courted her for several years. Everybody had said how well suited they were for each other and it was assumed that they would be wed – until fate dealt a cruel hand. Two winters ago Sarah had taken sick. Her rosy bloom quickly faded and the sparkle went out of her eyes. In a matter of days she had passed and William was left with nothing but emptiness. No other girl could ever match his Sarah and, although many girls since had given him the eye, William could not bear the thought of ever being unfaithful to the memory of her.

He paused for breath in the churchyard of St Bartholomew's, perched high on top of Chosen Hill. Finding Sarah's grave he placed a small posy of meadow buttercups on the damp turf and thought about his life. What was he going to do with himself? What prospects did he have? He was a Journeyman Carpenter, like his father Emanuel and his Grandfather before him, another William. In his Grandfather's day times had been good. There had always been demand for a good carpenter and wheelwright. Grandpa William had always kept meticulous records and had proudly shown young William, when he was first apprenticed, all the different kinds of work he could expect to work on; farm building repairs, tree felling, construction work, plough repairs, wagon and cart repairs, wheel repairs, fencing as well as the small domestic jobs that were always required.

William sighed and pushed back a lock of sandy hair from his eyes. He gazed down on the sunlit spires of Gloucester cathedral some miles distant. Where had it all gone wrong he asked himself? In a few short years the Gaze family had gone from being a thriving family business to the Poor Relief. How could a man like Emanuel afford to keep his family together on a handout of two shillings and sixpence a week from the Parish? There had been eleven children in the family but his sister Mary had died an infant some years ago and his other sister Charlotte was away in service. Yes, he and four of his brothers did bring in a little money each week but this was hardly enough to keep them from starvation some weeks. His mother Mary had had to beg the Parish for extra relief the other month just to buy clothes for the younger children. They gave her just seven shillings. It was simply that the work was no longer to be had. There had been three or four bad harvests recently and landowners and farmers had to lay off many of their labourers. Because of this much of the routine work of general farm repairs; tools, ploughs and buildings had dried up. The Gaze family were not the only carpenters in the village and now there wasn't enough work to go round. That was why he was off to the Hiring Fair this morning. Like many others he was hoping that some local farmer or landowner would take him on for the coming year. As a single man he would be given board and lodging as well as payment at the end of the year's service. It might mean putting aside his carpenter's skills and turning his hand to something else for a while but even that would be better than the shame of the Poor Relief and it would give the family one less mouth to feed.

By now the path leading down the hill towards Hucclecote was filling up with other young, and not so young, hopeful men and a few women. Just as William carried his carpenter's tools each carried a badge of their trade; shepherds carried their crooks, cowmen a tuft of straw, dairymen and maids carried their milking stools. William fell in step with the growing silent stream. A few nods of recognition were exchanged but each was lost in their own private thoughts.

William was jerked from his own thoughts by the sound of running feet and a cry of, "Hey Billy boy! What you'm doing then?" Turning to the question he was met by his younger cousin George, son of his father's brother, yet another William. The Gaze family seemed to have a distinct lack of imagination when it came to naming! Fresh faced and with the same sandy hair and steel grey eyes of all the Gaze men, George was just twenty years old and full of himself.

"On the way to the Fair then are we?" he asked. William nodded. "For what good it's worth" he muttered, half to himself.

"You'm becoming just like your Pa", laughed George, "a grumpy old man. You know what your trouble is Billy boy? You'm old before your time, that's what. You needs to get yourself a good woman."

William felt his fists begin to clench and the anger

begin to rise in him but George continued, oblivious to the signs.

"Perhaps you should buy yourself a wife at the Fair. I heard over in Andover the other year a bloke did just that. He sold his wife to the highest bidder. You might get yourself an old maid. That'll put a smile on your face Billy boy!"

William tried to contain his anger. "That's not funny", he snapped. "Just because you're courting that Elizabeth Hiccups don't mean give you the right to be so damned happy about life."

"What's not to be happy about on a morning like this eh?" continued George. "This time next year I intend to be married and I'll have a good job, because I'm young and ambitious. Where will you be eh? Stuck in the same old rut as ever, still not married, still no job – and still on Poor Relief!"

William's anger was reaching exploding point. His fists clenched tight and his steely eyes began to flash danger. But before he could retaliate George clapped him on the back and vaulted the stile ahead. "I'll see you around Billy boy and I wager that I'll get hired long afore you do."

George's laughter echoed in William's ears as he disappeared. His words had stung him and his mood blackened with each step towards the Fair. The trouble was that George had said true, he was becoming like his father, he could see it in himself already. He had to do something; something to get him out of this never ending rut

William climbed the stile deep in thought. It was not that he was unintelligent. His father had insisted that he learn to read and write before becoming an apprentice and he had received a basic education in the village schoolroom down near the Green. In fact he had shown himself to be quite bright and the schoolmaster had once told him that he should be setting his sights a lot higher than just becoming another 'door mender and coffin maker', as he had put it. At the time William had just laughed, becoming an apprentice carpenter and working for his father was all he had wanted at the time but now he was beginning to realise the truth of that statement. That was what he had become, a door mender and a coffin maker. Where was the skill in that? Seven years of apprenticeship just to make a box for a dead person? He was better than that! William had also read quite widely, that was another problem. He read everything that he could lay his hands on. The Bible and Prayer Book was the staple fare at home but William loved to read books and especially newspapers when he could get hold of them. He liked to think he knew what was going on in the world, certainly more than his cousin George who seemed to look no further than the constrictions of his own limited life! Recently William had read some writing by a William Cobbett in a weekly broadsheet titled the 'Weekly Political Register'. Some people had referred to these sheets as 'Cobbett's Twopenny Trash' but

William identified with what Cobbett was writing about. He wrote about the impoverished conditions of the agricultural labourers in terms such as 'their dwellings fall below pigsty standards and their food not nearly equal to that of pigs', something that William could well understand. Cobbett also advocated the emancipation of the poor and the more of his work he read, the more William found himself agreeing with these sentiments and several times in the 'Hare and Hounds' he had voiced his opinions, a little too forcibly sometimes. So much so that some of the older men in the village had branded him a radical thinker and suggested that maybe he would be the leader of the next revolution. Is that what it would take to make things better for the poor – a revolution?

Head down and lost in thought, William followed the other men into the field on Dacre's Farm. The Hiring Fair opened up before him. The field was already full of people, mostly men but a fair few women as well he noticed. There was a general air of gaiety and festivity amongst the crowd but even with the sun shining down it could not disguise the fact that these were all desperate people looking for work. The local farmers and landowners were stationed around the perimeter of the field; some sat in carriages, some on carts whilst others just stood and shouted their needs. William jostled through the crowds. He nodded and half smiled at a few men he knew but with every rejection he received he felt less and less like smiling. Not even the promising winks of a few pretty girls could lighten his mood.

He was drawn towards a corner of the field where a large man was standing in an open carriage loudly addressing the gathering crowd. William pushed his way forward to the front.

"Come all you likely lads and listen to me", called the man. "You are all good honest workers I know but how many of you have found work today?" A muttering passed through the crowd, clearly many hadn't. "Then listen to what I can offer you", he continued. "Do you want the opportunity of earning a decent wage?" A few shouts of 'Yes' and 'You'm damned right' rose from the people behind him. "What about if I offered you more than a decent wage with the possibility of being a landowner in your own right as well?" A cheer rose from the crowd at this and a few even applauded. "Then listen to what have to tell you. If you are a craftsman or a skilled labourer, then Mr Thomas Peel Esquire needs your services to build a new Colony in the distant land of Australia. You sir", and he pointed straight at William, "what's your trade sir?" William swallowed and answered
"Journeyman carpenter sir and a wheelwright."
"Carpenter and wheelwright eh? An excellent trade sir and one that will be well valued and rewarded in the New World", this barker continued. "And for

your service this is what Mr Peel offers you. For a period of indentureship he will offer you passage to Australia. He will offer you a more than generous wage with board and lodging and, what is more, at the end of your period of indentureship each man will receive a package of prime land in Australia to do with what he will, with no let or hindrance. In effect gentlemen, you will, after a period of time, become landowners in Australia! Now what do you say to that?" The crowd remained silent and for a moment the barker looked confused. Then the crowd began to break up, some laughing in derision others just shaking their heads in disbelief. Australia? Was this man mad? Who would leave their homes and families to set off to an unknown world? Only a few remained, including William. The man regained his composure. "Come now my lads. Mr Peel can't say fairer than that can he? What have you got left for yourselves here in England eh? Poverty and the Poor Relief? Come to Australia where you can be free men. Come on, who will take one of my leaflets?" and he held out a fistful of broadsheets. Without thinking William reached out and took one. It read;

> **SWAN RIVER**
> **WESTERN AUSTRALIA**
> **FREE PASSAGE** for single and married craftsmen
> and labourers and female domestic servants
> willing to sign indentures.
> Assistance reward actual money costs of passage is
> being granted
> by the agent General to Farmers, Dairymen, Market
> Gardeners
> and others desirous of obtaining Freehold Farms
> with Rich Agricultural Land
> in this part of Australia
> Farm Labours Single men 17 to 35, married up to
> 45
> and single women Domestic Servants 17 to 35, may
> obtain
> **FREE PASSAGE**
> Thomas Peel Esq. accompanied by Mr Smart,
> Gloucester (the local agent)
> will hold a
> **PUBLIC MEETING**
> And to be in attendance at the following place from
> 6 to 10pm
> **The New Inn – Gloucester**
> **On the 26th October**
> To answer queries, see applicants personally, and
> issue forms.

"So, my bonny lads" continued the man, drawing

the remaining few closer to his carriage. He sensed that he had captured their attention now. "For those of you who are seriously interested, Mr Peel's agent will be in Gloucester two weeks hence for you to make applications and sign the necessary paperwork. Don't you forget now, this is the opportunity of a lifetime that Mr Peel is offering you. This could be your pathway to the future."

William walked away rereading the broadsheet. A new future? Wasn't that what he wanted? To get away from the poverty of Churchdown and be the man he wanted to be; to spread his wings and make something of himself?

"What you got there then Billy boy? Not been listening to that old clap trap have you?" George appeared out of the crowd and stood before him, grinning from ear to ear with his Best girl Elizabeth on his arm. She smiled sweetly at William and it reminded him of Sarah.

"Got yourself some work then?" George goaded.

"No" replied William

"Told you I'd find work afore you didn't I? Farmer Bayfield has taken me on over at Upton St Leonards for the next year and, now that I've found work Lizzy has agreed to be my wife. We're off to see her Pa right now and I'm going to officially ask for her hand."

"Congratulations to you both", William forced a smile for Elizabeth. "I am sure you will be very happy."

"And what about you William?" purred Elizabeth, "what are your plans?"

The broadsheet burned in his clenched hand. "Me?" he said determinedly. "Me? I'm off to Australia!"

CHAPTER TWO

February 1829

In the oak panelled study of the London residence of Thomas Peel the two men sat opposite each other, across the open fire, in earnest conversation. Thomas Peel, the younger of the two men, took a sip of his whiskey.

"I think you should know before we proceed any further that I have just had word from the Colonial Department that they have brought forward the deadline." The other man, Solomon Levey, raised an eyebrow.

"How so?" he asked.

"No reason was given but isn't that always the way with this Government? All they say is that in order to have claim on the first two hundred and fifty thousand acres of land along the Swan, the first shipload of settlers must have arrived by the first of November this year."

Levey wetted his forefinger and ran it thoughtfully around the rim. " And can you realistically meet their demands?" he asked quietly.

"I don't see why not", Peel replied, "The Gilmore is already chartered and will leave London towards the end of July. I've met with her Captain and he assures me that, even with putting in to Plymouth to pick up myself and my family and other settlers from the West Country, we should be at Swan River by the end of October. Three months at sea should be adequate."

"And the other ships?" mused Levey.

"The Hooghly and the Rockingham are due to sail later in the year with additional provisions and the rest of the settlers. By mid way next year we should have upwards of four hundred settlers in place. And, of course, you have promised to ship additional provisions from your base in Sydney."

"Yes, of course", Levey said almost dismissively with an idle wave of his hand, "but what happens if you miss the deadline set?"

"I will forfeit the right to my first two hundred and fifty thousand acres. I have been informed, instructed rather, that the Lieutenant Governor, Captain James Stirling, will allocate that land between the small number of settlers already there."

"Then you had better ensure that you do arrive on time", said Levey, "I would hate to think that my investment in this scheme depended purely upon the whim of the weather!" Levey's voice carried just enough threat to make Thomas Peel swallow hard. The older man locked eyes with Peel and held his gaze just long enough to affirm the threat.

Solomon Levey was a shrewd businessman. He had already spent a number of years in Australia in New South Wales building from nothing the merchant company of Cooper & Levey, which was based in Sydney. He looked at Peel again who was gazing thoughtfully into the fire. He recognised greed when he saw it; he had seen it in Peel's eyes when they had first met. Levey had done his homework well and knew all about Thomas Peel. Son of a wealthy cotton manufacturer in Lancashire, Peel was impatient to wait for his inheritance. With an older brother in the Church, Peel was disinclined to follow his father into the business and lived on a generous annual allowance. He was a chancer, Levey knew that, always out for the easy life. What was it someone had once said about Peel? He had ambitions far beyond his station. Yes, that summed him up well. Until recently Peel had lived with his wife and three young children on an estate in Scotland but now he was reduced to this more modest residence in London. Levey broke the silence.

"You do realise that the Swan River is totally unknown land as far as you are concerned, don't you?"

"Yes, that's the beauty of it," replied Peel. "Alright, I know Captain Stirling has charted the area and its surrounds and that he has a small garrison and settlement there but the Colonial Department now want to develop a Crown Colony there, with private funding. It's new virgin territory we will be settling." His voice betrayed his greed. "And I, we, will be in at the beginning. Think what this will mean for you as well. A new base for Cooper & Levey on the west coast of Australia."

It was a good point Levey had to admit. If, and only if, Peel's plans worked out then Cooper & Levey would have the monopoly along the western coast. But it was a risk, he also knew that. Then again, he thought to himself, he hadn't got where he was today by not taking a few risks. A former shipping clerk, transported to Australia in 1815 for theft, he had served his time, become an Emancipist and then used his skill and knowledge to develop the company. He had known what hardship was, especially being a Jew as well, and he knew how cut-throat business could be. Peel knew nothing, he was a dreamer. His first plan to ship settlers to New South Wales would have worked admirably, had not the other members of his syndicate dropped out! But when the Government put forward the proposal for opening up Western Australia Peel had jumped in with both feet, sensing the opportunity to become the landed gentry that he desired to be. It was only when Peel had turned to himself for advice that he had realised just how financially insecure Peel actually was. Levey was to invest a significant amount of money over a ten year period with Peel as his partner, although Peel in effect would become a salaried 'Manager' in the new settlement.

Peel downed the last of the whiskey from the glass that he had been cradling in his hands and placed it on a nearby table. "So we are in agreement then?" he asked.

"Yes, I believe so" came the measured response. "I will provide you with the financial resources to the first four hundred settlers to Swan River. You will provide the finances, from whatever source you can," he added somewhat acidly, "to provision the initial settlement. I will undertake to reprovision you from Sydney during the first year of settlement. In return for all of this investment you will grant Cooper & Levey merchant rights in and out of the new Colony, yes?" Peel smiled and nodded in agreement.

"Yes, agreed." And he stretched out his hand towards Levey. Levey did not respond.

"Agreed then, but I have two stipulations if I may?" he asked.

"Yes?"

"Firstly, that this scheme must be seen as your sole endeavour only. My name should not appear on any correspondence from you to the Government. The fact that I am a former convict and also a Jew I fear would not go down particularly well in some quarters and could jeopardise the entire venture. I therefore suggest the company be named as the Thomas Peel Company."

Peel nodded. "Agreed."

"And secondly," Levey continued, "that all indentured labourers, craftsmen and domestics be paid in promissory notes issued in the name of Cooper & Levey. These should be used to pay for provisions provided by my company or can be redeemed for money at your own expense. If you agree to these two terms then we can proceed with the venture."

Peel hesitated for a moment at the thought of paying his labour force 'at his own expense' but, as that seemed most unlikely, he nodded. "Agreed!" he sighed. Then, and only then, did Levey shake his hand.

A gentle knock sounded on the study door. "Come!" called Peel and his manservant Johnson entered quietly.

"Begging your pardon for disturbing you gentlemen but Mr Peel sir, you did ask me to tell you when it was half past the hour. Your guests are assembled for you in the Drawing Room and dinner will be served in half an hour sir."

Peel stretched and stood up. "Thank you Johnson, we shall be down presently. We are finished here I think?" He looked pointedly at Levey.

"Indeed we are Thomas," smiled Levey, "I won't detain you from your guests any longer and I only hope that your offer to them proves acceptable."

"Are you sure you will not stay for dinner?" asked Peel, "I am sure there is ample to accommodate another at table. Is that right Johnson?"

The servant nodded. "Without a doubt sir. One more place can be accommodated quite easily."

"No, thank you Thomas, I won't stay, I am quite sure. In any case the more invisible I am the better for our plans eh? It would not really do for us to be seen as partners, at least not as yet". Levey's steely eyes demanded no reply and he made for the door. "I will be in touch regarding the movement of funds to your Bank by the end of April."

"Thank you indeed", responded Peel, "Johnson, would you see Mr Levey to the door please?"
The servant bowed ever so slightly. "Of course sir. Mr Levey, if you would follow me please."
The two men walked down the stairs together not saying a word. At the foot of the stairs they parted silently, with a nod and a final handshake, Levey to disappear into the February night and Peel to his guests in the Drawing Room.
"Gentlemen, welcome to my home. I trust I have not kept you all waiting for too long?" Assembled in the Drawing Room were twelve well known landowners from the counties around London. Peel had carefully selected each one and they had been honoured to have been invited to dinner in London at the home of such an illustrious person as Thomas Peel, of the wealthy Peel cotton family. But, as yet they were uncertain as to exactly why they had been invited. Peel beamed magnanimously and nodded to Johnson. "Gentlemen, let us not wait upon ceremony. Please, go through to the Dining Room. Johnson, the doors please." Johnson pulled open the double doors that led to the Dining Room and the guests passed through, each taking a place at the immaculately laid table with Peel at the head. He waited for the drinks to be poured before raising his glass and calling for a toast the 'the King'. The men responded in full and then fell upon the first dish. Courses came and went and the drink flowed freely. The conversation around the table ranged from the price of livestock to the political intrigues of the day

but Peel avoided all mention of Australia. The time was not right, yet.

At the end of the meal Peel reached forward and tapped the rim of his wine glass with a knife to attract attention. The conversation subsided and all eyes turned to him. Burdened by the efforts of excessive dining he hauled his somewhat portly figure to a standing position and surveyed the room. "Gentlemen", he began, "you will by now, I am sure, be wondering why I have brought you all here this evening. As much as I have enjoyed the pleasantry of your company at dinner I must confess to having an ulterior motive." The guests looked at one another, agreed puzzlement on their faces. "Allow me to explain", continued Peel, "Britain, Great Britain, this country we love so much is in crisis. Agitators, propagandists and radical thinkers are fermenting trouble for us landowners. Unrest is spreading through the land and we are in serious danger of the masses revolting against us." Some of the guests nodded in agreement. They too had read the pamphlets and newspapers. They too had experienced this 'growing unrest' to which Peel referred. Some, especially those from Kent had received threatening letters from a so named 'Captain Swing'. "So Gentlemen, this evening I am about to extend to you an offer that is beyond your dreams; an offer that will allow you to build the Utopia we dream of so much". Peel was now in full flow. He might lack a degree of business acumen but he was, by any measure, a good speaker.

"By now most of you I am certain, will have read reports of my scheme to establish, in conjunction with His Majesty's Government, the Crown Colony of Swan River in Western Australia. I have, only very recently, received confirmation from the Colonial Department that this scheme is to go ahead and I can inform you all here this evening that the first ship, the Gilmore, will sail at the end of July."
A gentle cough came from the listening men and a voice sounded from the other end of the table.
"Er….Mr Peel, excuse me for interrupting but who exactly will be funding this venture?"
Peel paused momentarily, his mind straying briefly to his conversation with Levey earlier in the evening.
"A good question sir and one that should be rightly asked. I personally will be funding the shipment and provision of the first four hundred settlers."
"So the reports in the newspapers concerning your cousin's involvement with the scheme are wrong then?" came another unprompted question. Peel flushed with anger.
"Those reports sir are damned lies!" he thundered. "The Home Secretary, Sir Robert Peel, is a distant relative of mine, which is a fact well known it seems. But in no way at all did I use my family connections to influence a Government decision in my favour!"
"Then you did not ask the Home Secretary to write to Sir George Murray at the Colonial Department to intercede on your behalf, as reported?" continued

the man.

"No sir! Not at all! I may have, at some function or other some time ago, mentioned my proposals to him in passing but I can assure you that no correspondence whatsoever has passed between him and myself concerning the matter!"

Another voice was raised. "You know Mr Peel, don't you, that the press are now dubbing you the 'The King of Swan River'?"

"What those scandalous rumour makers choose to call me is immaterial to me. The scheme that I have proposed to the Government, that the press now call 'The Swan Job', has been accepted on its own merits. The Colonial Department has seen the sense in establishing a Crown Colony at Swan River backed and developed by private funding, not convict labour as in New South Wales." Peel began to regain some of his composure. "This is the way forward gentlemen. This is the way to build the new Utopia and you too can be a part of that. I am in a position this evening to offer you prime agricultural land along the banks of the Swan River at the knock down price of only one English pound per acre. This land is suitable for both arable or livestock farming. It is freehold land and will be yours to own outright."

The gathered group of landowners looked at each other. One pound per acre? That was a ridiculously cheap price for virgin land. There had to be some sort of catch, it was too good to be true.

"And how much land is available?" came a question.

"I am selling the land in plots of one thousand acres. So for one thousand pounds you will receive one thousand acres. That's more land than some of you own now."

"And what about livestock?" asked another.

"Provision can be made to ship your livestock with you, subject to a space limitation of course, should you engage in this offer. I say space limitation because we need settlers there before we have the livestock. We can't have a Crown Colony settled by cattle can we?" Peel smiled and a few men laughed with him.

"But what about the people who live there already?" continued the voice.

"There are a few settlers there but they live mainly in the area around the garrison."

"No, I mean the native people". The room fell silent at this and all eyes turned on Peel.

"I am not sure I fully understand your question sir. The native people? They are just natives. I am reliably informed by Captain Stirling that he finds them most amenable."

Peel had not anticipated this line of questioning. "Won't they mind losing so much of their land?"

"Sir", Peel went on the attack, "you are talking like a radical. These are native people sir. They don't own the land, they just live on it. By settling the land we are offering them a chance to become part of a civilised society. Captain Stirling has already talked about some who now work for him. Why should they not work for us as well?" Peel felt that he was regaining control of the situation. "So again gentlemen I say to you this is an opportunity not to be missed. If you do, and I am sure that you will, accept this offer then I have certain small stipulations to the offer." A murmur spread throughout the men. "The first is that you have to personally settle your land in Australia. The second is that for every one thousand acres of land purchased under this scheme you must undertake to fund the passage of ten other settlers other than yourselves. Your passage and that of your families will, of course, be free."

"And when must we decide on this?" asked a man. "Gentlemen, it would be most unfair of me to expect an answer this evening. I can see that several of you are interested but you will need time to think the matter through I am sure. I shall be here in London for the next week and, should you have any further questions, I will be only too pleased to discuss the matter further with you individually. In the meantime if you could let me know your intentions within seven days hence we can conclude the business most efficiently." Reaching behind him he gently tugged a bell pull and, almost instantly, Johnson appeared in the doorway.

"Johnson, my guests will be leaving shortly. If you could arrange for their coats please?" Johnson bowed again almost imperceptibly and left, as silently as he had arrived.

"And so gentlemen, I will bid you all a good evening and I look forward to receiving your decisions soon." Leaving the room he gleefully rubbed his hands together and smiled to himself. His dreams of becoming a wealthy landowner were beginning to come true.

CHAPTER THREE

June 1829

     William sat outside of the family cottage sharpening his tools. The early summer sun shone down warmly and birds were busy flying in and out of the thatched eaves. A high hedge shielded William from prying eyes in the lane as he laid out the tools on the ground before him; chisels, saws, brace and bit, augers, mallets and all the other accoutrements of the journeyman carpenter. The wooden handles were polished with years of use. Some of them had belonged to his Grandfather, passed on to him before the old man had died. "Take care of these tools boy," his Grandfather had said to him, "take care of them and they will see you right no matter what." He picked up a chisel and felt its balanced weight in his hand. What would the old man have had to say about him now, he wondered?

     It had been several months since that William had announced that he was going to Australia. He had ridden over to the New Inn on Northgate Street in Gloucester at the end of the last October and made out his application as instructed at the Hiring Fair. Mr Peel had, seemingly unusually, been at the meeting himself, a rather overweight and pompous individual William had thought, but his enthusiasm was unquestionable. Appearing on an upper balcony he had spoken for some moments to the waiting people, standing below in the cold open courtyard, after which there were a few questions and then William joined the line of men and women waiting to make application for passage.

When it came to his turn William was able to fill out the required form and sign it for himself, unlike many others who had dictated their information and made their mark, a simple cross in the required space. Peel's agent in Gloucester, a Mr Smart, who was dealing with the applicants turned to Peel and commented, "We'll have to be watching this one sir, an intelligent one this. A carpenter who can read and write!" Peel fixed his eyes on William who returned his gaze, saying nothing. In that moment both men acknowledged each other and knew that their paths would cross again at sometime in the future.

It was only after William had signed and committed himself that he had felt able to tell the family. He had known that had he told them of his plans beforehand, they would have done their damnedest to make him change his mind. Now that he had signed there could be no turning back, no matter what was said. As luck would happen the day that he had decided to break the news to them was the day that his brother Edwin's shoes had finally fallen apart. Over the meagre evening meal of broth his mother Mary had asked his father if there was any money spare to buy him a new pair. Emanuel had exploded in rage, "Damned children! All I ever seem to do is to have to find money for them! Do I look as if I've got any money to spare?"

"But the boy can't do without shoes, can he?" pleaded Mary.

"Shoes is expensive", thundered Emanuel, "it's enough that what little I brings in just about feeds us. I put a shaft on a cart and two spokes on a wheel last week, is all. And what did that bring me in? One shilling for the shaft and one and twopence for the spokes. How can we live on that and find money for shoes?"

Mary said nothing, she just looked at William and then at the other children and motioned for them to eat their broth and stay silent.

"We'll have to go cap in hand to the Parish again and beg them for money for his shoes I suppose", continued Emanuel. "It cuts me hard to have to beg like that. You don't know what it does to a man!"

William put down his spoon in exasperation. "Pa", he said, "it's not begging. If a man is in a position where he can't look after his family, through no fault of his own, then of course he should look for help."

"I've been an independent man all my life, just like my father and his father before him. I've worked hard for this family and I don't need telling from my own son what is right and what is wrong!"

snapped Emanuel.

"Pa, you're not the only man in this position", replied William. "There are other men in Churchdown, all over the country even, who haven't got enough food to put on the table, enough money to clothe their children. It's like Cobbett says, the poor live lower than the pigs they tend."

"Cobbett! Cobbett! I'm sick of hearing this revolutionary radical clap trap! It's all well and good him writing about how bad it is for us poor but when is he going to DO something to help the poor? Eh?" Emanuel was flushed with indignation and he gestured wildly at William. "You'm turning out to be nothing but a free thinking radical and if you can't say anything sensible in my house then you may as well leave!" Spoons clattered into bowls and mouths dropped open. The other children stared first at their father then at William and finally their mother. They had never heard their father speak like this. William drew breath and paused for a moment, looking at his mother.

"Then maybe I will." He answered quietly. His father seemed not to have heard him and continued, "Sometimes I rue the day I encouraged you to read and write. What good has it done you eh? Oh aye, you can read your Bible and Prayer Book but what other rubbish have you filled your head with eh? Propaganda, radicalism and revolution! Aye, revolution! That's what I've raised, a revolutionary!"

"Emanuel, please", snapped Mary, "the children, please!"

"Enough woman! You'm no better either, encouraging him in his ways. You just tend the children, is all!" Mary's eyes glistened with held back tears. One or two of the younger children whimpered and ran to hide their faces in her skirts; they were frightened of their father's sudden angry tirade. She gathered them to her as a mother hen would her chicks. William's anger flashed and he rose from the table, standing tall over his father.

"You leave Ma out of this", he warned, "she does her damned best for you and for us. I've seen her make her fingers bleed stitching and darning by candlelight well into the night just to make clothes last that little bit longer. And where have you been eh? Down at the Hare and Hounds complaining about how little work there is. You mayn't have much work but you can always find a few coppers for a mug of cider!" Emanuel sprang to his feet, his face now purple with rage.

"What! Don't a man deserve a mug or two at the end of the day? Since when have you become a so high and mighty Puritan? Something else you've read is it? By God! I didn't raise you for this. I wanted you to be educated so as you could do something with yourself. Make something of your life!" It's now or never, thought William.

"Then maybe I have. I'm leaving for Australia."

His words fell like a sledgehammer. Nobody moved, frozen in the moment. It was as if some artist had come along and painted a portrait entitled 'the family at war'. Silence hung heavy and it was his mother who was first to break the tableau, her hands went to her face and she began to weep openly, no longer able to hold back the pent up tears. All eyes turned to William and then to Emanuel. William suddenly felt a great elation as if a heavy burden had been lifted from his shoulders. "I am going to Australia Pa", he said quietly, "there's no more to be said. I've already signed the indentures to travel to the Swan River. I'll be leaving this July."

Emanuel Gaze seemed to fold in on himself, gasping for breath. Like a punch drunk prize fighter he reeled and then collapsed into his chair. "But……..why?" was all he could manage. All fight had gone out of him now.

"Because of this, the way we are", explained William calmly. "Because there's not enough work to go round; because I'm just another mouth to feed; because we have to ask for Poor Relief. I know it's hard for you Pa but that's the way this country is going. You've seen the way things are changing. We've already seen threshing machines that can do the work of a few good men. How long before other new machines will be doing other jobs and put more men out of work? How long do you think wheelwrights will last when they've started using these new metal wheels? The poor will always be poor, unless they do something for themselves and that's why I am doing this. What's left for me here? The craft is dying let's be honest. It's like the Reverend once told me, we will become coffin makers and door menders before long. Is that what you want, because it's not for me? My life is empty here since Sarah passed. I need a new start." He went over to his mother and put his arms around her shoulders. He could feel her frailty as she tried to control her weeping. "You gave us all that you could. You made sure I could read and write, have a trade but now it's time for me to do something for myself, to make a better life in Australia."

That had all been several months ago. William placed the chisel with the other tools on the ground and took up a saw. Since that evening his father had barely spoken to him and his mother seemed to have fallen into some state of mourning for her lost son. They had even asked the local vicar to try and dissuade William from leaving but, whilst feigning sympathy for his parents, when speaking alone with William he had understood and supported his decision. He had hated hurting his parents in this way but it was what had to be done. Within a few months they would realise that he had made the right decision for the family.

His thoughts were interrupted by a whistle and a cry of "Hey Billy boy!" Looking up from his work he was greeted by the sight of cousin George and his fiancée Elizabeth at the garden gate.

"So this is it then, is it?" began George, "Thought we'd stroll over the hill and say goodbye to you afore you go."

"That's good of you George; Lizzy. I'm glad that you did. How's life in Upton these days?" Elizabeth flashed a smile at him. "We're making plans for the wedding, aren't we George?" George mocked a grimace and Elizabeth gave him a dig in the ribs. "Take no notice of him William. He's as excited as a young puppy. It's such a shame you won't be there though." And again she smiled.

"No, sadly I shall be many thousands of miles away but I am sure all will go well without me being there and, if I can remember, I will raise a glass to you both on the day. Between the Gazes and the Hiccups I am sure you will have such a crowd that I won't even be missed."

George gestured at the laid out tools. "Getting ready for the off then are we?"

William nodded. "Aye, just making sure that all my tools are in good shape. I'll be relying on these to see me through the next few years. My trunk is all packed, not that I have that much anyway, just these to sort out and then I'm ready.

"When do you leave?" asked Elizabeth. William stretched in the warm sunshine.

"Day after tomorrow. Down to Gloucester Docks, then a barge on the new Gloucester and Berkley Canal down to Bristol. From there I'll pick up a carrier down to Exeter and then on to Plymouth. Should take me but a few days."

Elizabeth clapped her hands. "It's so exciting. Such an adventure. I wish I was coming with you".

George shot her a disapproving look.

"I'll wager your Ma's upset" he said, quickly changing the way the conversation was going.

"Aye, she is, that's for sure. But I'm sure that when I've gone she will be as right as rain again after a few days. The young'uns will keep her busy".

George nodded. "After she lost your Mary she spent all of her time and efforts on the rest of you. I suppose she feels that she's losing another child. How's your Pa now?"

William sighed a long deep sigh. "If only he'd talk to me, is all. He cuts me dead when he sees me and the only time he does speak is to demand his pipe or something. I don't want to leave him in this way. I want to leave with his blessing."

"Well I'm sure he will come to his senses before you leave", said Elizabeth. "We're on our way to see your uncle Solomon. I'll ask him to have a word with his brother. If anyone can make him see sense he can."

"I'd appreciate that Lizzy, although I don't think it will do any good. But thanks for trying anyway. Maybe when I've gone he will realise how much he meant to me. I'll write of course but I don't know how long a letter will take from there. I'll write to you two as well if you like."

"Please" said Elizabeth, "and you can tell us all about your adventures and those infamous blackmen who live there. I've seen drawings of them in a book", her voice dropped to a conspiratorial whisper, "they don't wear any clothes you know!" She blushed and giggled and she demurely covered her mouth with her hand whilst looking up at William through half lowered lids. George tweaked her hair and laughed, although he gave William a fleeting hard look.

"Enough of that Lizzy. You're nearly a married woman remember. Bring your imagination back here, you shouldn't be having thoughts like that." William began placing the tools in his canvass bag tool bag.

"So", sighed George, "I suppose this is it then? I'll shake your hand Billy boy and wish you well. We haven't always seen eye to eye in the past I know but I wish you no harm. We'll part as friends eh, as well as relatives?" and he extended his hand. William clasped it firmly and then, spontaneously, the two men hugged each other.

"You take care of yourself Billy boy, you hear me? And you come back safe some time." George whispered in William's ear.

"I will", replied William with a catch in his voice. Each man's eyes were moist with unshed tears. William tried to make light of the situation. "And you look after young Lizzy here. You've got a diamond there George. You don't deserve her. If I wasn't going away I'd be having her away from you!"

George laughed, "Billy boy, if she's too good for me then she's definitely too good for you!"

Elizabeth stepped forward and placed a kiss on William's cheek. "This is for you William. I will miss you." Her warm scent and the softness of his lips upon his skin brought old memories flooding back to him. Emotion rose in his throat.

"And I will miss you" he whispered as she pulled away and turned to follow George through the garden gate. And, as she did so, for a fleeting moment William gazed upon his Sarah's face. A tear finally broke and trickled from the corner of one eye as George's "Be seeing you Billy boy!" echoed down the lane and then they were gone.

"And I'll miss you both", sighed William.

CHAPTER 4

July 1829

The carrier reined in his horses. "I'll drop you here sir, if I may?" he said.

The horses steamed in the early morning sun and shifted restlessly between the shafts. William jumped down and hauled his black wooden trunk from the back of the cart.

"That's alright Thomas, many thanks for the ride." He reached into his waistcoat pocket and took out a handful of coins. "I think this was the agreed price?" The old man took the coins readily and counted them one by one into his pouch.

"That's right sir, as agreed." His leathered face, weather beaten over many years, cracked a toothless smile. "Just follow the road young sir, pass the hospital and you'll see the Citadel below you. The port's there sir, near the dockyards, you can't miss 'em".

William nodded as he shouldered the trunk and picked up his precious canvass tool bag.

"Safe journey Thomas and thanks again".

"You too sir. I don't envy you, all that way over water in a wooden box. Give me a pair of horses any day!" A throaty chortle crackled from his throat as he settled into his coat and flicked the reins. The horses responded immediately, heaving against the weight of the cart. "Good luck to you young sir, I don't envy you at all."

The cart picked up a steady pace and branched off left, leaving William alone at the side of the road.

He breathed deeply in the warming sun. Already he could smell the tanginess if the sea and the cries of the sea birds seemed to call him on. This was the first time William had actually been alone since he left Churchdown ten long days ago. His farewell had been tearful, as he had known it would be; his mother and the younger children had wept openly. Only his father remained unmoved, standing resolutely in the doorway. William had embraced his mother, brothers and sisters and then turned to his father.

"No word Pa?" he asked

The two men faced each other, eyes searching for answers.

"I don't want to leave it like this Pa, but my mind is made."

A fleeting shadow passed the older man's eyes as he struggled to find words.

"You'm a grown man now son. You'm made your own life", was all he said and slowly he extended his hand. William blinked back the tears. This was finally the acknowledgement he had wanted; he had needed. He grasped his father's hand with emotion. "Thank you Pa."

And then he was gone. He didn't look back. He didn't want to because he knew that he had to cut

the cord. His Uncle Solomon had offered to ride him into Gloucester Port in his cart and as they trundled through the village neighbours and friends came to their gates or called out from the street;
"Good luck William"
"Safe journey Billy boy!"
"Don't forget us."
The two men sat side by side, unspeaking, each lost in their own thoughts, all the way into Gloucester.

In the shadow of the Cathedral, Gloucester Port was a bustle of activity. Ships were being loaded and unloaded. The opening of the new canal two years previously now meant that ships no longer had to be dependent upon the tides to negotiate the river Severn from Bristol up to Gloucester. The new canal also meant that small fast barges called fly-boats could cover the thirty or so miles in less than twelve hours and it was on one of these that William had booked passage.

Solomon reined the horse to a standstill. Like his brother Emanuel he was man of few words but he turned to William.
"Well boy, this is it for you. I wish you a safe passage and good luck in your new life, wherever it may lead you. Don't you forget us now back in Churchdown. I'll look after your Ma, don't you worry. Come back safe some time eh?" He thrust a hand at William. It was a carpenter's hand, calloused and scarred from years of working with wood. William had never really noticed it before

but now he seemed to be seeing everything
with fresh eyes. He shook his Uncle's hand and,
with a final nod, the two men parted.

William walked around the canal basin
where long narrow boats were being loaded and
unloaded. He was looking for the fly-boat named
'Sarah Jane', a good omen William had thought. He
stopped and asked some boatmen where he could
find Captain Jones and his boat. He was pointed to a
far wharf where the 'Sarah Jane' was being loaded
with timber. Captain Jones welcomed him warmly
and ordered the boat boy to help William down into
the forward 'passenger' cabin with his trunk. Many
fly-boat captains took the occasional paying
passenger as a means of supplementing their
income. As William dropped down the narrow
hatchway in the small forward deck into the dark
wood panelled box that was to be his cabin he
wondered if he would have more room on the ship
to Australia. He poked his head out into the sunlight
again and watched the loading being completed. A
canvass cover was stretched across the loaded
timber between the forward cabin and the crew
cabin in the stern. Three boatmen and a boat boy
crewed the 'Sarah Jane' and one of the men hitched
his horse to the fly-boat and the boat boy unhitched
the mooring ropes and pushed off before jumping
aboard. With surprising ease the fly-boat began to
move forwards as the horse settled into a steady
pace. Captain Jones settled at the tiller whilst the

two other men walked alongside the horse. The boat boy disappeared into the crew cabin and soon smoke appeared from the blackened metal chimney as he stoked the stove. Before long William and the other men were presented with steaming mugs of tea. The time passed gently. Sometimes William walked the towpath with the other boatmen, helping with the two locks that had to be negotiated along the way. The boatmen seemed to take these devices for granted but William marvelled at the ingenuity of raising and lowering the level of water in the canal. 'Progress', he thought, 'it's coming fast and can't be stopped'. The tranquil journey passed uneventfully and, before long, the fly-boat hauled into the Sharpness basin where suddenly tranquillity exploded into organised chaos. There were boats everywhere, of all shapes and sizes, and the noise was overwhelming; the endless rumbling of cart wheels and the constant shouting of boatmen and carriers.

William collected his belongings from the cabin and with a brief farewell to Captain Jones and the crew he threw himself headlong into the tumult in search of a carrier heading towards Exeter. Asking around he soon found one prepared to take him as far as Tiverton for a reasonable fare. From there he had managed to pick up with the carrier Thomas who had taken him up over Dartmoor and down towards Plymouth.

Churchdown seemed so very far away now

already. William paused in the morning sun and rested on his trunk, taking in the vista below. He had reached the ridge and as the road dropped away he could see all of Plymouth laid out before him. The sun sparkled on the open sea that stretched away into the distant haze and the sounds of a busy port rose up towards him. From the dockyards he could pick out the familiar sound of mallet against wood and the rhythmic rasp of saws. The gentle knocking of boats against the stone wharves mingled with the flapping of sails and the sighing of the breeze through rigging. He surveyed the Lilliputian scene; nothing was still, there was a constant movement. Ships and vessels of all kinds were moving in and out. Others were moored off shore whilst small skiffs flitted between them, their oarsmen moving like clockwork automata. Like swarming ants sailors clambered amongst the rigging. Sails were being furled and unfurled, whilst on the dockside carts were endlessly coming and going and even more were being loaded and unloaded, their patient horses standing like statues in the warm sunshine. Even in the Citadel, the heavily defended fort that protected the dockyard of Devonport, red-coated soldiers paraded in miniature like the wooden toys that William had played with as a boy.

William breathed deeply. His lungs filled with fresh sea air and he felt alive, full of a sense of adventure and new beginnings. He shouldered the trunk once more and set off down the hill with a jaunty step wondering which of these fine ships below was the 'Gilmore'. Swinging along at a steady pace, whistling a catchy tune he passed the Military Hospital at Stonehouse Creek where some of the inmates were taking the air in the grounds. They waved and acknowledged his happy demeanour. Crossing Stonehouse Bridge he made his way into the town, heading towards the newly named township of Devonport, the dockyard area. The noise, the sounds and the smell avalanched over his senses. If he had ever thought Gloucester was a busy place then Plymouth was in another league altogether. Horse drawn vehicles of all descriptions crowded the streets and everyone seemed to be hurrying everywhere, heads down intent on their own business. Sailors and soldiers, resplendent in splashes of blue and red, mingled with the drab crowd. Some had bottles in hand and girls on their arms, whilst from darkened doorways other girls beckoned after the single men. A few even called after William, suggestive gestures making their intentions quite clear, but William declined their invitations with an embarrassed smile. The air around him was thick with the pungent and acrid stench of unwashed humanity. Filth from the streets mingled with the odour of industry; the stench of the tanneries, breweries and fishing sheds. Almost suffocating in this overwhelming miasma William headed for the sound of the sea, seeking fresh air to breathe.

The town of Plymouth merged into Devonport without obvious notice and William sought the Embarkation Depot on the dockside, as he had been instructed. Not sure what to expect he was directed to a large wooden building where lines of men, women and children were queuing to get into the Embarkation Depot office. William joined the line of waiting people behind a family of seven and wearily he dropped his trunk to the floor and sat on it. He observed the group before him; the older man, about fifty years of age, he presumed to be the father, a stocky individual with the reddened face of a man who had worked outdoors all of his life. The mother, if indeed she was for she seemed so young, had delicate features under her bonnet and dark eyes that glanced at William. He looked away hurriedly, suddenly conscious that he was intruding. Perhaps she is an older daughter, thought William, although as she nursed the younger child she displayed the clear intimacy of a mother. The five other children ranged from a broad shouldered boy of around seventeen years down to the nursed child of around two, or so William thought.

"Is this the right place to be for boarding ships?" he asked.

The older man looked at him. "It is young man. You might be waiting awhile though. We've been here for some time already, haven't we my dear?" The wife-daughter nodded. "Where are you for?" he asked.

"Swan River, Australia" replied William.

"Then it is a small world", laughed the man, "for we shall all be shipmates as that's where we are bound as well. Thomas is the name; John Jacob Thomas, but call me Jacob And this is my wife Emily." William shook hands with the man and acknowledged his wife with a smile.

"And these are my children", Jacob continued, "John the eldest at sixteen, then there's Thomas, Jane, Edwin and our little Emily." The children all nodded at William respectfully.

"William Gaze, carpenter" offered William in reply.

"Travelled far William?" asked Jacob.

"Gloucester. It's taken me ten days in all."

"That's a fair way to come", said Jacob, "We've travelled a distance too, from South Wales ". William laughed.

"I suppose that will all mean nothing compared to how many miles more we have to travel. So, Jacob, what takes you and your family to Australia then?" Jacob sighed and looked at his wife. "I had a smallholding just outside of Cardiff, livestock mainly. Then we had a bad winter and we lost most of our stock and then the rents was put up. When you've worked on the land all your life what else is there to do? There's no future for the children so I saw this notice about farmers being needed in the new Swan River settlement and so, here we are."

"Me too", said William. "I served my

apprenticeship as a carpenter but now there are too many carpenters in our village for the work available. And I can see the writing on the wall Jacob. It won't be too far in the future before machines will do many of the jobs that we used to do on the land, you mark my words. So, I thought, a new land; a new life. They'll certainly need my skills where we're going."

"Are you alone?" Emily spoke for the first time.

"Yes, sadly" replied William.

"Then we shall be pleased to look after you", she smiled again, "you can become one of our family if you wish, for the journey".

William felt an instant liking for the ruddy faced Jacob and his petite wife Emily.

"Then thank you" he replied "I wouldn't want to be a burden but it would be pleasant to have somebody to pass the time with on the voyage."

"Then that is settled" beamed Emily. Suddenly the line of people began to move. "John" she said, turning to her son, "help William with his trunk", and before he could protest John had easily hoisted his trunk onto his broad shoulder and moved forwards, William beside him carrying his tool bag.

"Surely not all of these are bound for Swan River are they?" he asked John.

"No" replied the boy, "need a damned big ship to take this lot." No, some of them are for the Americas, some for Asia and some are for New South Wales on the other side of Australia. They all have to report here and get their papers checked before they are allowed to board. You know we all have to have a medical check don't you?"

"Medical check? No" replied William.

"You've no worries, you look healthy enough" laughed John and William noticed that he had the same laughing glint in his eye as his mother. "As long as you've all your teeth and have not got any obvious illnesses they'll let you through."

The line crept steadily forward until at last they reached the Embarkation Desk. A bored and officious looking Clerk looked up wearily from a pile of papers on the desk.

"Name?" he demanded tersely.

"Gaze, William" responded William

"Where bound?"

"Swan River"

"Papers?"

William laid his Indenture papers on the desk and the Clerk peered at them from behind his grimy spectacles. He dipped his pen in the ink well and scratched a few words on a sheet of paper.

"On board the Gilmore. You embark tomorrow morning." A few more words were scratched and the Embarkation papers were signed.

"Here. Don't lose them!" He thrust the documents at William and gestured absently to his left. "That way for your medical. Join the line to the left. Next!"

And with that William was dismissed. He joined the

shuffling queue of men and boys waiting to be examined on the left side of a large screen. Women, girls and small children were being directed to the right hand side of the screen. The examination, when it finally happened, was cursory. William handed over his papers and a bored and rather unhealthy looking Doctor took his pulse and then listened to his breathing. He examined William's eyes and teeth before peering into his mouth and then asked some rather vague questions about 'how had he been in the last year?' Another piece of paper was signed and added to the growing collection that was handed to William and then he was free to move on.

Emerging into a further room William found himself in, what was to all intents and purposes, nothing more than a large wooden barn fitted out with rows of pallet beds and was clearly some form of dormitory.

"Over here William!" came a voice. He looked around trying to locate the owner of the voice amongst the crowd. "Over here!" shouted John Thomas again and waved at him. William pushed through the crowd. "Here, I've saved you this bed next to us. Might as well stick together eh?" William smiled and threw his canvass bag onto the hard mattress, claiming it as his own. The trunk he placed on the floor next to the bed. As he stood up fatigue suddenly rose up and hit him like a sledgehammer. He kicked off his boots and lay on

the straw mattress, his mind a vortex of images of
the last few days; the tearful farewell; his father's
words; his Uncle Solomon's calloused hands; the
'Sarah Jane'; the endless jolting cart journeys and
the teeming mass of humanity all bound for new
lives. Somewhere amongst this whirlpool of
thoughts sleep claimed him.

The morning dawned bright and clear.
Sunlight filtered through the high windows as
Embarkation Officers strode through the fetid
dormitory calling passenger names. William was
suddenly aware of being shaken.
"Come on, William. It's us. We've been called!"
Jacob was shaking William by the shoulder. Emily
was busy fussing over the children and John was
already hauling William's trunk onto his shoulder.
William hastily pulled on his boots, having slept
like the others in his clothes. People all around were
rubbing sleep from their eyes and doing the same, in
a rush less they should miss their embarkation.
"Here, let me" said William, taking the trunk from
John. "You help your mother with the children".
John relinquished the trunk and with just as much
ease scooped up the two younger children in his
arms. The large doors at the end of the dormitory
were pulled open and sunlight and fresh air flooded
in. The Thomas family and William followed the
others called for the Gilmore out on to the dockside.
The tall masts of ships rose all around them like
some strange alien forest as they were lead to the

ship that was to be their home for the next three months. The Gilmore loomed above them, its three masts seeming to disappear into the blue sky above them. The settlers filed up the steep and narrow gangway to the open top deck. The sight that greeted them was like something out of the Old Testament. Arranged on the upper deck, in pens and crates, was all manner of livestock; cattle, horses, pigs, sheep, goats and various poultry. The children's eyes opened wide with astonishment. Around the sides of the ship were bound bundles of straw and barrels of grain for fodder. Jacob turned to William

"Looks like our Mr Peel has set himself up as the new Noah. Look, here's his Ark!" he laughed. He cast a farmer's eye over the scene. "I only hope he keeps us as well provided. Mind you, keeping that straw out in the open won't do much good. A few drops of wet on that and it will soon rot!"

"Married couples with children under eleven follow me!" a sailor shouted.

"Single men and boys over eleven this way!" cried another.

"Single women and girls over eleven over here!"

There was much consternation and wailing as families were split up, unwillingly at times. Families were to be billeted mid-ship, single men and boys in the bows and single women and girls in the stern area, all below decks. Emily clung to John and Edwin as they were called away, John being sixteen and Edwin twelve. William placed a hand gently on her arm, "Don't worry Emily, I'll look after them. As if they were my own brothers". She smiled that warming smile at him again. "Thank you William, I know you will." And she held his eyes a moment longer than was necessary, William thought.

"Come on then boys, let's see if we can get bunks together" and with a nod at Jacob he led the two boys after the sailor. As they crossed the deck William glanced up at the Quarter Deck and recognised the portly figure of Thomas Peel in earnest conversation with the Captain. Peel happened to look round at that moment and saw William below. For a moment he held William's gaze before nodding at him in recognition. He leant on the rail "Gaze, isn't it" he called. "Carpenter if I remember rightly. Gloucester. Clever fellow. Reads and writes".

William nodded, surprised that he should have been recognised, and called "Yes sir, your memory serves you right indeed". Peel turned away before William could say anything more and continued his conversation with the Captain, although William did notice that Peel gestured towards him more than once and the captain gave him a hard look.

"Do you know him well?" asked John.

"Only as my employer" replied William thoughtfully. "I can't think why he should recall me so well."

"That could be a good thing – or a bad thing for you. He knows who you are!" said John as they descended the steep flight of stairs into the gloomy depths of the ship. William ran his hand along the oak beams. This was good timber, heart wood, well seasoned; he knew his timber. This will see us through, he thought.

The sailor led them forward to the single men's billets. The space was dark and cramped and already full of other male settlers who had joined the ship at London and Gravesend. Picking their way over piled belongings William and the two boys found spaces near each other and stowed their belongings in the allocated, if somewhat inadequate, space. A gruff older man, by the name of Murphy, watched them hawkishly from his pallet. He broke off from sucking on his pipe.

"Make yourselves comfortable me boys" he laughed "this is your home for the next few weeks". Home? Where was that they wondered.

At three o'clock in the afternoon, as the tide was rising, preparations were made for departure. William and the two boys met with the others at the dockside rail as they watched events unfolding. With much shouting and cursing mooring ropes were slipped as two skiffs began to tow the Gilmore away from the dockside. Oarsmen strained their backs as the large ship began to inch forward. Thomas Peel stood proudly on the Quarter Deck as Captain Geary shouted endless and seemingly unintelligible orders to the sailors. As the Gilmore eased away from its berth the gathering crowd on the dockside raised three hearty cheers for 'Mr Peel and the Gilmore!' Peel acknowledged the crowd, who waved back at him. The children on board, swept along in the ritual of departure, waved and cheered loudly, although many of the adults, William included, remained silent and thoughtful as land began to fall away.

Skilfully the Captain threaded the ship through the maze of moored vessels in the harbour as the dockside began, at first slowly and then more rapidly to slip away. On reaching the Sound sailors expertly climbed the rigging and, inching their way precariously along the yard arms, began to unfurl the sails. The tow skiffs loosed their cables and, as the sails began to fill with the wind, Captain Geary headed the Gilmore out to sea. William watched silently as the English coast, his home, slowly but steadily disappeared into the afternoon haze.

CHAPTER 5

August - September 1829

The settlers assembled silently on deck in the grey morning light. Rain was gently falling as befitted such a melancholic occasion as the tiny bundle, wrapped in a chain, was dropped into the sea. A muffled sob was the only sound as Mr Peel and the Captain, standing on the Quarter Deck, replaced their hats and turned away. A few women went to comfort the grieving father and lead him away. During the night George Inkpen's wife had gone into labour, earlier than anticipated. The ship's Doctor, Surgeon Lyttleton, had attended her in the female infirmary but despite all his best efforts the child was stillborn. Hastily baptised by the Clergyman it had been thought best to dispose of the body quickly, hence the early morning funeral. There had been no prayers or words spoken; George had forbidden it, just a tiny bundle of cloth dropped into the sea; the first of many over the next few months.

It had been almost two weeks since the Gilmore had left Plymouth and the excitement and novelty of being at sea had now given way to the monotony of shipboard life. The daily routine never varied; breakfast, dinner, supper punctuated by long periods of inactivity. Wash days were Wednesdays and Saturdays and clothes lines were strung between the main masts where the freshly laundered clothes had flapped in the constant stiff breeze. They reminded William of the Rag Fairs back home. Sundays, at least, were a break in the routine. A Clergyman on board mustered the settlers and crew for prayers and hymns and although not particularly religious William, like many others, went along willingly to relieve the boredom.

The weather so far had been fair, according to the sailors, and a steady breeze had driven them ever southwards, the sails straining with the unseen force of the wind. William had grown accustomed to the constant pitching and rolling of the ship. Unlike some of the others he was not alarmed at the creaking and cracking of the ship's timbers as she ploughed through the waves. As a carpenter he knew that wood had to be allowed to bend and give with the movement. Also, unlike many of his fellows, he had not succumbed to the dreaded sea-sickness. Both John and Thomas had spent several days lying on their beds alternately heaving into a pail that separated their bunks. Some of the other men, equally afflicted, didn't even bother and spewed into their beds or directly onto the floor, until the acrid stench of stale vomit was almost too much to bear. Nothing could be done for them except to encourage them to sip fresh water and sleep. As it was strictly forbidden for women to enter the single men's accommodation Emily had been unable to visit her two sons. In spite of her protestations the First Mate had been adamant and no amount of female persuasion would bend him. By the end of the first week or so most of the afflicted had recovered sufficiently enough to strip their pallets and sluice out the quarters with drawn buckets of sea water. It was commonly thought that Alice Inkpen's early labour had been brought on by her having suffered by sea-sickness.

The gathered settlers had now dispersed. Emily, standing next to William, took his arm. "I want to thank you William for looking after the boys. It has been a great comfort to me". William smiled at her, unsure of what to say. "It's strange isn't it" she continued, gently steering him away from the rest of the family, "I feel as if I have known you all of my life and yet we have barely been together for these two weeks past." William looked across at Jacob who smiled and waved at them. He felt comfortable with Emily on his arm, her nearness aroused long suppressed feelings within him, and yet he felt confused. He felt the attraction but she was Jacob's wife; Jacob's second wife to boot! He had confided as much to William on the third night as they stood at the rail together gazing out across the sea. They had stood silently for some while before Jacob spoke. "You know Emily is my second wife don't you?" he had said unexpectedly. William chose his words carefully.

"I did think that might be possible as she is seemingly younger than yourself".

"She is barely past thirty years of age, significantly younger than me! At fifty two I count my blessings to have found such a devoted mother to all of my children."

William remained silent, sensing that Jacob wanted to unburden himself further.

"I married quite late you know" he continued "about your age I would say. Mary was her name and she gave me two strapping sons, John and Thomas. But Thomas was a difficult birth you see and Mary took sick. The fever took her quickly." He paused and looked out over the sea. "What was I to do eh? A babe in arms and a four year old? My parents were both dead and Mary's mother had passed on before she had even married me. Emily was our servant girl for three years. She adored John and took to the new baby as if it was her own. I asked her to marry me shortly after Mary's death. Was I wrong William?"

"You did the best for your two boys Jacob. Who can say that is wrong? And she bore you three more children, who she appears not to favour any more than John or Thomas."

"I know William," nodded Jacob, "I know. I couldn't have asked for more from her but…..but sometimes I see her looking at younger men and that makes me feel my age. You understand what I

59

mean William?" And he gave William a strange look, not accusatory but meaningful enough. William hesitated for a moment, searching for diplomatic words.

"If I am ever fortunate enough to meet such a woman as Emily then I am certain that I shall feel as you do." Jacob nodded and said no more.

And yet here he was only a few days later, arm in arm with a married woman barely a few years older than himself and she was clearly flirting with him! He turned to her.

"Emily, listen, I know….."

His words were cut short as a sailor high above called

"Land ho! On the leeward!"

All the remaining settlers on deck rushed to the leeward rail, peering at the distant horizon. Slowly a patch on the horizon darkened slightly and then grew more steadily to become an obvious land mass. Thomas Peel appeared on the Quarter Deck and looked down on the excited crowd of settlers now thronging the port rail to catch sight of the first land they had seen since leaving England.

"Ladies and gentlemen" he called "That which you see over yonder is the island of Madeira. We are now well on our way and to celebrate our good fortune and the improvement in the weather Captain Geary has agreed that this evening we shall have singing and dancing".

A cheer went up from the crowd at the prospect of

some light relief and a change in the routine. Emily squeezed William's arm.

"You will dance with me, won't you William?"

And before he could make a reply she had skipped back to Jacob and the children, leaving him in even more confusion.

By mid afternoon the sea had grown flat calm and now only a breath of wind eased the Gilmore on her way. The air had grown noticeably warmer and ready hands cleared a space for the festivities on the main deck between the livestock pens. Each Mess of six passengers pooled their provision of Pork, Peas and Potatoes and the ship's cook began to prepare a wholesome stew. At dusk all were assembled and as the sun slipped below the horizon the sound of concertina, fiddle and whistle echoed across the empty sea. Captain Geary had declared that every man should receive a glass of grog, a much welcomed treat, and Mr Peel and his son, so rarely seen above decks, sat together with the Captain on the Quarter Deck enjoying the entertainment. Feet stamped and petticoats whirled as the settlers, in a sudden burst of exuberance, allowed the pent up emotions of the last two weeks to be released.

William leant against the rail, the grog sending a warmth coursing through his body. Although he did not see her he sensed Emily's presence. She touched his arm and he flinched as if stung.

"What's wrong William? Won't you dance with me?" she whispered.

William looked across the deck. John was dancing with one of the single women, Thomas was playing along with the musicians and Jacob was sat laughing with the other three children, feet tapping in time with the rhythms.

"I know you want to" and she pressed closer to him, her body warm and willing against him.

"Is it wise Emily?" he asked "You're a married woman. Jacob's a friend of mine, you all are."

"So. Can't friends dance together?"

"You'd be better dancing with your husband."

"Pooh, Jacob!" she tossed her hair and snorted "He can't dance, or he's forgotten how to. William, I want to dance. I want to feel like a young girl again. When I am with you that's how I feel. You make me feel like that." She rose on her toes and turned her face to kiss him. William firmly held her by the shoulders and stopped her. He could feel her shoulders trembling beneath her thin shift.

"Put it from your mind Emily. I can't deny that I think a lot of you".

"I know you do" she said breathlessly and pressed closer into him, "I know you do. I feel it in you every time I come near you. I can feel it now"

"Emily, whatever I may feel for you inside can never be anything more than that; a feeling inside. You are married to a good man, with five lovely children and you are sailing to a new life together.

Don't let this ruin what you have and ruin my friendship with Jacob and your family. I respect you all too much for that. I value you as friends. And we will all need friends where we are going."

Emily subsided and rocked back on her heels, stifling a muted sob. A tear glistened in the corner of her eye.

"I thought you…."

"I know" said William gently, "I know. And now it's time for you to go to Jacob." Gently he lowered his head and his lips brushed the crown of her head. "Go to your family."

Emily turned and walked away without further word. As William watched her go he caught Jacob's eye and the two men nodded at each other, both fully aware of what had just passed.

The days grew warmer and longer but with the increasing temperature came a noticeable lack of progress. The air had grown still and there was barely a breeze to be had and the sails hung limply from the yards. In the growing heat the settlers became listless, even more listless than their usual routine dictated, and it was not uncommon to see men stripped to the waist and women with their skirts hitched up. The heat began to affect the livestock also. The cattle in particular were becoming dehydrated and fresh water was running low. Some of the owners were sacrificing their daily water ration of three quarts to supplement their beasts. Some sheep and pigs had been lost in the earlier bad weather and now it looked as if the cattle might follow.

Tensions began to grow between both settlers and crew. Several games of Crown and Anchor had erupted into violence and on one particular hot and humid night Henry Forward had been sliced in the arm. William and John had been watching the game between a group of sailors and some of the settlers. Quite a lot of money was exchanging hands and Henry seemed to be losing heavily. Suddenly accusations of cheating were being thrown around and before anyone knew what was happening a blade flashed and Henry was clutching his bleeding arm. The playing mat and dice were scattered as sailors and settlers squared up to each other. William and John held back the angry sailor with the knife before any more damage could be done. The sudden explosion of noise on an otherwise peaceful night brought the Duty Officer and men quickly onto the scene. The sailor was arrested and Henry taken to the infirmary to be stitched up. The next morning a summary Court of Enquiry was convened by the Captain and Thomas Peel. Statements were taken from all who had been present, including William and John, and a decision was quickly reached. The sailor who had attacked Henry was discharged from duty and placed on bread and water for the rest of the voyage and the Captain forbade any further games of Crown and Anchor, although some illicit games still took place deep in the bowels of the ship.

The skills of Surgeon Lyttleton seemed to be more and more in demand. As the Gilmore approached the Equator, or 'the line' as the sailors preferred to call it, the heat grew so intense that they could have cooked steak on the deck, had they had any. Several of the older women fell ill of the heat and were confined to the female infirmary in the stern of the ship. Two of them had died quickly. Those younger women that were nursing young babies became so dehydrated that their milk dried and three of these children had died. Death was now not uncommon and accidents increased as the heat made everyone more careless, especially the children. Broken bones were common and several children had broken arms or legs by falling through hatchways left open to increase the ventilation below decks. Edwin himself had narrowly escaped a nasty fall when playing on deck at Fly the Garter. Only William's timely hand had grasped the boy's arm to prevent him from falling headlong down the open fore hatch.

William now spent more time with John, teaching him the basic skills of carpentry and wood working. Between them they whittled dolls for the girls and a complete set of wooden soldiers for the boys. He had tried to avoid being alone with Emily since that evening off the coast of Madeira, not such an easy thing to do in such a confined space; it was difficult to be alone anywhere on the ship. He was still friends with the family but there was now an underlying tension between the three adults.

The arrival of the Gilmore at 'the line' gave occasion to lighten the tensions all round. On that morning, some thirty days into the voyage, a slight breeze had picked up and the ship had begun to make headway at last. Schools of porpoises played around the bow wave and flying fish were now a regular sight. The porpoises were too agile to be harpooned but some of the sailors managed to catch a five foot long shark, much to the astonishment of some of the settlers who marvelled at the rows of sharp teeth as the shark thrashed on deck before being dispatched by a sailor. The shark meat was to make a welcome supplement to their now meagre diet of preserved pork and peas. All the settlers were mustered on deck, the men not being allowed to shave, much to their puzzlement. The sailors, dressed in an array of unlikely costumes grabbed a passenger, one Frederick Lipscombe, blindfolded him and brought him before 'Neptune'. Asked where he was from the man opened his mouth but, before he could speak a word, a pill of tar was pushed into his mouth by another sailor. Gagging, he was immediately dowsed with a bucket of water, much to the delight of the crowd below. Calling for the next passenger William suddenly found himself being thrust forward by the younger children. Playfully protesting he allowed himself to be blindfolded and lead up the steps to the Quarter

Deck. Mindful of what had happened to the previous victim when asked where he was from William kept his mouth firmly closed. At this a sailor dressed as a Doctor pronounced loudly that this passenger needed a draught and, ordering his mouth to be held firmly open, a pail of sea water was poured in. The children clapped and cheered and then the Doctor pronounced that the passenger was clearly very ill and needed smelling salts. A burnt cork studded with needles was then placed under his nose, causing him to yelp in surprise. Beads of blood welled up on the end of his nose. Then having been found guilty of not speaking to Neptune when asked the sailors lathered his face with muck and tar before shaving him with a piece of tin. To complete his punishment he was then tipped headlong into a barrel of sea water. The crowed laughed and cheered as William emerged from the barrel holding the blindfold aloft in triumph. John and Thomas ran forward to help him from the barrel and carried him over to the family.

"You're a fine man William" laughed Jacob. "Not many would have borne that with as much grace as you've done!"

"Did I have a choice?" replied William. "Edwin and the others were not exactly going to let me get away with it, were they?" He glared playfully at the three younger ones who giggled with mock embarrassment.

"You should all be ashamed of yourselves!"

snapped Emily, and as their faces fell she added, with a wink at William, "But it was so funny!" And they all laughed, including William.

"Here, let me." Emily took a cloth and wiped some of the tar from William's smarting face. He raised his hand as if to stop her, afraid that this intimacy would rekindle past events but she brushed his hand away. He caught Jacob's eye.

"It's alright William. Let her. It's alright now." As other settlers were tarred and dowsed with water and the crowd hooted in delight, there in the quiet corner of the deck Emily gently bathed his face and he knew then that theirs' was now a friendship built on trust and not desire.

The ceremony of 'crossing the line' was concluded with glasses of grog issued all round, a feast of shark meat and yet more music and dancing. This time William did allow himself to dance with Emily but it was he who asked permission of her husband and they danced freely and unabashed, secure in their friendship.

The days passed and as the Gilmore slipped steadily southwards the weather began to change. It grew colder and the wind began to pick up. Squalls were now commonplace and rain raked the decks like grapeshot. As the seas grew steadily rougher and water began to wash across the deck the Gilmore rolled and pitched. Settlers struggled together to build barricades to protect the livestock from the worst of the weather, lashing whatever spare canvass and timber together to create windbreaks. Sailors clambered aloft to take in the main sails, leaving only the smaller top sails to drive the ship forwards. The sea and sky leaked into one steel grey panoply. With darkness came no relief, only fear. Some of the more religious settlers set up prayers as they feared they would soon be drowned.

William lay on his bunk listening to the painful creaking of the ship's timbers. The wind outside was now a shrill shriek and with every plunge forward the Gilmore took he could hear the roar of the sea breaking across the bow. Sleep was impossible; men were thrown from side to side in their bunks with every lurch of the ship. Anything that was not lashed down or stored securely rattled around the quarters.

With one tremendous lurch the Gilmore shuddered and the sound of a distant splintering rent the air and made William sit bolt upright.
"What's wrong?" cried John
"Not sure, listen" replied William, already pulling on his boots. Shouts and running feet could be heard above them. The Bosun's cry of "All hands on deck!" could be heard through the maelstrom.
"Come on," cried William, pulling on his coat.
"We're needed!" John and a few others grabbed their coats and hats and ran from the quarters, bouncing from side to side as the Gilmore rolled alarmingly. Pushing open the forward hatch a blast

69

of wind and water hit them. What they beheld, when at last they could see, was a scene straight from hell. The Main Topgallant mast had splintered in the storm and was swinging loosely by its sheets, scything across the deck like a giant pendulum. Ripped canvass was cracking in the wind and sheets flailed everywhere. With every roll of the ship water broke over the rails and cascaded across the decks. Sailors were hauling on ropes, trying to control the swinging broken mast. As William and the others clambered out onto the deck a huge wave crashed across the amidships and they watched in horror as a complete pen of cattle was swept away into the darkness. Dodging swinging ropes and shackles they scrambled for the remaining livestock. Some other settlers were already there, desperately trying to lash down loosened timbers.

"What can we do?" shouted William, his words barely audible.

"See to the livestock if you're able" came the reply, half carried away on the wind. "Save what you can!"

Another wave broke and William watched in disbelief as the man, unbalanced for a moment, was plucked by the torrent of water and carried away. His mouth emitted a silent scream as he disappeared into the blackness beyond. Cattle and horses were rearing and plunging with every roll of the ship, unable to keep their footing in the torrent of water around them. Some were already dead; others were lying with broken bones unable to stand. The shriek of the storm mixed with the screams of the frightened animals.

"The dead and injured will have to go!" shouted William.

"What?" mouthed John.

William leaned closer. "Help me cut the dead and injured beasts free. We need to put them over the side!"

John nodded his understanding, the storm ripping away their words. Speech was useless; signs and gestures became the new language. Clinging desperately to any hand hold that they could the two fought their way across the deck, timing their movements to the rolling of the ship. Drawing knives from belts they slashed at the tethers of the dead beasts and watched as, with the next rush of water, the bodies were carried over the side. Oblivious to the danger and immune to the cries of the frightened animals, they slashed at leather and rope, freeing both the dead and injured to be washed overboard.

The Gilmore lurched wildly, out of rhythm and a rush of water raced across the deck.

"John! Watch out!" William's words were ripped from his mouth as a dead cow, swirling freely in the torrent struck John in the back. He lost his footing and, holding only the tether of the dead animal he was swept towards the rail and the dark void beyond. William lunged forwards after him. His actions were instinctive; he had no thought for himself, only for his friend. As beast and boy were washed towards the rail William's hand caught John's belt. He slammed into the rail but held fast. Bracing both of his feet against the rail he clung desperately to John's belt, praying it would hold. Every muscle strained against the elemental forces as slowly the ship began to roll the other way. With one heave William pulled the now senseless John across the rail and onto the deck. The ship began to roll again but this time William was prepared. Holding tightly onto John he wedged them both tightly into the corner of a pen where it had been securely fixed to the deck so that the seas broke over them but did not carry them away. With every back-washed roll of the ship William lashed himself and John together and then, cradling the unconscious boy from the worst of the storm he prayed the night would end soon.

CHAPTER 6

November 1829

"This is absolutely intolerable!" Thomas Peel rose from his chair and slammed his fist down hard, glaring across the desk at Captain Geary. "We have been in port now for over six days and I don't see sign of any imminent departure. When exactly do you plan on resuming this voyage?"

"May I remind you Mr Peel", replied Geary calmly, "that I, under the terms of the Ship's Contract, am entirely responsible for the seaworthiness of this vessel. Considering the amount of damage and loss of life that we incurred during the storm I would have thought you would have been only too pleased to make it as far as Cape Town in one piece. My carpenters are doing their very best to make all necessary repairs and we will not sail until those repairs are carried out to my complete satisfaction and I have engaged further crewmen to replace those who were lost. If you are not happy with these arrangements then you are at liberty to charter another ship out of Cape Town."

"You know damned well there are no other ships available in port at this time!" Peel blustered.

"Then you must be patient for a little while further Mr Peel. We will get you to Swan River I assure you."

"But I should have been there before the beginning of November, you are aware of that. It is in the Contract. We are already into November and as I am now not ashore by that deadline I will forfeit land grants."

"I am fully aware of that Mr Peel and I will endeavour to reach our goal with all due speed. However, I can not be held responsible for delays caused through storm or tempest. You may challenge that if you wish but I am sure that any English Court worthy of its name would not hold any Captain responsible for an Act of God! I would however be held accountable if I were to lose my ship through being negligent in maintaining its seaworthiness! Now, if there's nothing further I have work to do." Geary rose from his chair and fixed Peel with a glare that challenged him to continue this conversation further, if he dared. Geary hesitated long enough to allow Peel to respond.

"No? Then I will bid you farewell for the moment. I will report on the progress of the repairs this evening." He turned on his heel and left the cabin.

"Damn!" Peel swore and sat down heavily in his seat, thinking hard.

It had been six days since they had limped into Table Bay and the port of Cape Town after the storm. The damage had been considerable; two of the upper masts, he could never understand their proper names, had been snapped off and the bow jib had also been broken. Several of the sails had been badly torn and some of the rigging had had to be cut away and lost. The morning after the storm, when the wind and waves had subsided enough for people to venture out on deck, the ship was a sorry sight. Splintered timbers and a tangled mess of ropes littered the decks. The livestock had been decimated; pens and cages had been swept away wholesale. Much of the poultry had simply disappeared. Peel reckoned that about two-thirds of the beasts had been lost; either killed during the storm or, being so badly injured, had been slaughtered afterwards. Only the bloodstock horses had fared reasonably well. Peel had insisted at the outset of the journey that these animals be kept in specially constructed stalls under cover off the main deck with specially constructed slings and harnesses to protect them against the pitch and roll of the ship. One or two had had to be slaughtered because of injury, much to his chagrin, but the others had all survived; enough for a decent hunt, he thought. The one positive thing arising out of this loss of stock was that some of the slaughtered beasts were now being butchered and the meat preserved for the rest of the voyage.

There had been loss of life as well. Five crew members had lost their lives during the storm. Two had been seen to be washed overboard and one died the next day from injuries received when a falling mast had hit him. Two other crew were unaccounted for, presumed dead. The passengers had also suffered casualties that night. A roll call taken the morning after showed seven dead; two men had been washed overboard; one woman had died of sheer fright and the other four had died of crush injuries received below decks; two of those four had been children. It had been a cold and bleak funeral service as Captain Geary, in the absence of the injured Clergyman, committed the six canvass shrouded bodies to the deep and held a memorial for those whose bodies had been lost. Many others had been injured and the more serious cases, William and John included, were now in the infirmary. Surgeon Lyttleton's resources were so stretched that other settlers were helping to nurse the sick and injured.

Peel sighed deeply and drew paper and ink towards him. There was a Barque bound out of Cape Town for London tomorrow and it was important to send letters to both Levey and the Colonial Department. He dipped his pen and began the first of his letters;

Cape Town
November 4th

My dear Levey,

Calamity has befallen us! Eight days since we encountered the most fearsome storm one could imagine. The Gilmore suffered much damage and there has been a significant loss of life. More importantly, much of the livestock has been lost.

We are currently in the port of Cape Town being refitted before continuing on to Swan River. I am endeavouring to restock and reprovision as best I can but decent livestock is hard to come by here. It is <u>imperative</u> that you send additional stock and provisions on the next available ship.
Captain Geary is confident that we will reach Swan River by the end of the month. I wish that I had his confidence for I fear that we may arrive too late by far and therefore lose our full land grant.
I pray to God for a fair wind.
I remain yours
Thomas Peel.

Peel dusted the letter and read it through. He did not want to elaborate further but he hoped that Levey would realise how vital it was to send further stock and provisions as soon as possible. Peel hoped that the Hooghly had not yet sailed and that Levey would be able to take on additional supplies. He folded the letter and sealed it before drawing another sheet of paper towards him.

Cape Town
November 4th

Sir George Murray
Secretary of State for War and the Colonies
The Colonial Department

Dear Sir,

  I beg leave to inform you that we have made good progress on our journey to the Swan River.

  Such has been our progress that the Gilmore has briefly put into Cape Town to take on fresh water and provisions. Our good Captain Geary has taken this opportunity yesterday to marry the daughter of my Civil Engineer, Mr Benjamin Smythe. The passengers are therefore in high spirits and very much looking forward to establishing the new Colony at Swan River. There is a very positive air about the ship.

  I, and our Captain, have every confidence that we shall arrive at our destination with all good speed and I shall inform you of such in due course.

  I remain your humble servant,
  Thomas Peel Esq.

He dusted the letter, folded and sealed it and then addressed both letters. Calling his servant he instructed him to take both letters and hand them to the Duty Officer on board the barque 'Superior' lying in port. It was very important that these letters be handed directly to the officer and not some other crew member, did he understand? These were official letters addressed to His Majesty's Government. The servant nodded and left.

Peel sat at his desk gazing out of the window. He sighed again, his situation was becoming difficult. He knew that his grant of land along the Swan River was now in jeopardy but he also knew that Captain Geary was not a man to be pushed. Peel could not bully him as was his wont. Peel knew that Geary was right, the ship could not sail until completely sea-worthy, that was a fact and in any case being in Cape Town had allowed them to take on fresh provisions, even if that had been costly. The port side merchants had certainly had their pound of flesh out of him! Putting into port had also given everyone on board a welcome rest. His own son Thomas had been unwell for most of the voyage so far and had been confined to their cabin. Now, at last, he was able to walk freely on deck in the warm sunshine. For the first time in many weeks he had seen his son smile. He thought briefly of the passengers below decks, his passengers, and he wondered how they were faring. He stood and pulled his waistcoat straight. Perhaps he should make a visit to the infirmary?

The familiar sound of hammering and sawing filtered through the fog in William's head. He stirred and immediately a shaft of pain speared his left shoulder.

"William" A distant voice was calling him, a

woman's voice.

"William" came the voice again. His eye-lids flickered and he was dazzled by the bright sunlight that bounced around the room. He tried to focus as a blurred face moved closer to his. He was conscious of a warm scent that he vaguely recognised.

"William? Oh, thank God! Jacob, he's awake."

A second face appeared above him. He moved his mouth but no sound came. He ran his dry tongue along his cracked lips and managed to whisper hoarsely, with effort,

"Sarah?"

"No William, it's me, Emily"

"Emily?"

"Yes, you remember? Emily and Jacob? On board the ship to Australia?"

His mind fogged again and he closed his eyes as he struggled to remember. A soft hand was placed on his forehead.

"Poor lamb. You've been asleep for over a week now. Since the night of the storm. But you're back with us now."

Ship? Storm? Emily? Slowly and painfully images formed in his mind, like pieces of a jig-saw coming together, to form an incomplete picture. He made an effort to move.

"John?" he rasped. Gentle hands restrained him.

"Now lie still. It's alright now William. John's fine, all thanks to you. He's in the next bed asleep."

William struggled to open his eyes again. Slowly

Emily's face came into focus. Behind her stood Jacob. Both looked relieved.

"Emily" he croaked.

"Try not to speak. Here, take a sip of this water" Tenderly she cradled his head and raised the beaker to his dry lips. The water tasted cool and sweet and he took a second sip.

"Not too much too soon" said Emily, gently patting his lips. "You've been very poorly. We thought we'd lost you. You need to rest now."

Thoughts raced through his head. He was aware that there was a stillness in the room and that he could not hear the familiar sounds of the ships timbers creaking and groaning.

"Where am I?"

"You're in the infirmary" said Jacob. "There was storm, do you remember?"

"Storm? …..yes" Flashes of mountainous seas and a night of terror raced across his mind.

"Where are we now?"

"In Cape Town" replied Jacob. "The ship was in a bad way after the storm and the Captain had no choice but to make for the nearest safe haven"

"I think I remember…… the seas were washing over everything….the cattle were…..I saw a man disappear into the dark….John was…..!"

The pain came again as he tried to sit up.

"Let me help you". Jacob's strong arm supported him as Emily placed a cushion behind him. William sank back into the softness and tried to look around him. He was in the male infirmary in the stern of the ship. Sunlight flooded in through the open cabin windows and the air was fragrant with the scent of land. There were a dozen or so beds made up in the infirmary and all were occupied by male settlers; some asleep, some just sitting silently in their beds. William looked at the bed next to his and recognised the figure of John.

"Is he….?"

"He's fine now" said Emily, a catch in her voice. "When we found you that morning we thought we had lost him, lost you both. You were lashed together in the corner of the deck, as if dead, your arms cradling his head in the fold of your coat. John had a bad gash in his leg and was barely conscious. Jacob carried him down here and the Doctor stitched his leg. He regained consciousness quite quickly but you we couldn't revive. You lay in this bed as if dead, yet you weren't because you were still breathing." She began to weep quietly and Jacob picked up the story.

"John was able to tell us what you did. You risked your life to save his. Without you John would not have survived that night, wouldn't be here in fact. You shielded him from the storm at a cost to yourself. We brought you down here and Emily has cared for you both these last eight days."

"Eight days!"

"You have been out of this world for all that time. But you're back with us now, that is the important thing."

"My left shoulder pains!"

"You've had a nasty break. When we found you the bone had pierced the skin and was sticking out. The Doctor is a good man, he splinted and strapped it well. It will heal with time but you must be patient." The door to the cabin opened and the figure of Thomas Peel was framed in the doorway.

"May I come in?" he asked.

Jacob and Emily stood respectfully, surprised at this unannounced appearance.

"Of course, Mr Peel, sir. Please do." Jacob stepped aside to allow Peel to enter.

"I thought I would come and see how the patients are faring. Ah, Gaze! I see you are finally awake!" William was not sure if this was just an observation or an admonition.

"Yes sir"

"You are a hero sir, do you realise? I would shake your hand sir….but maybe at a later time eh?"

"Thank you sir but I am no more a hero than any other man that night."

"Well, that's as maybe I am sure, but you did save another man's life did you not?"

"I only did what any other man would have done sir" William paused, and then blurted out, "I saw a man die that night."

"Ay, yes, that is regrettable it has to be said. But those that died did not die in vain, some of the livestock was saved, and in no small part to your own heroic efforts."

William slowly raised his eyes to fix Peel's. "I'd rather those men alive now and lose the cattle sir. Do you place the value of your stock above that of your settlers?"

There was a sudden tension in the air. All eyes looked at Peel, sensing that William had challenged him, in spite of his condition. Peel coughed uneasily and looked around.

"Yes, well, we have all embarked upon a dangerous journey into an unknown world," he began, "and we are all in this together. We are as one family on this ship. Your suffering is my suffering; your loss, my loss and every loss is greatly felt, whether it be man or beast."

William's eyes blazed. The pain in his shoulder was nothing to the pain that Peel's words now caused. He made as if to speak but Jacob's voice diplomatically cut across his rising anger and he caught Jacob's slight warning shake of the head.

"I am sure Mr Peel, sir, we are all grateful for your visit but the patients here ought to rest sir and not be agitated in any way, especially about the night of the storm. I am sure that you will understand that the sooner they recover the more use they will be to you."

Peel was astute enough to realise that he had been given the opportunity to retreat with some remaining dignity before the situation could turn nasty.

"Yes, well then, I will bid you all a good day and I hope that you all make a speedy recovery." He nodded at Jacob and Emily and then, with a final hard stare at William, he left. William looked at Jacob.

"Why did you do that?"

"Because you are in no fit state to take on your employer in a battle of words."

"I had him there Jacob! I had him nailed to the mast. We all know now where his priorities lie. I wanted to hear him say it!"

"And what good would that have done?" asked Emily.

"Possibly not that much, but it would have made me feel a damned sight better" smiled William wanly. "Now help me out of this bed."

"William, no!" objected Emily.

"I need to take a leak. It's either going to be in that pail over there or I will piss in this bed! God knows how I've managed these last few days!"

"Oh, we've managed" said Emily quietly, slightly blushing. William raised his eyebrows and looked at Jacob.

"Jacob, your wife is nothing but a hussy! Now, for God's sake, give me a hand and get me over to that pail!"

Emily eased him gently into a sitting position and then Jacob helped him unsteadily to his feet. With the faltering steps of a new born colt William was assisted to the pail where he managed to relieve himself, conscious of the woman in the room, although Emily appeared not to notice. Feeling fresher he then cajoled the protesting two to dress him and to take him out into the sunshine. Jacob first checked on John, who was sleeping soundly oblivious to what had just passed, and so supported on both sides by his good friends William took a few unsteady steps out onto the deck. He sat gratefully on a nearby barrel and surveyed the scene.

The ship was a hive of activity. Men were working feverishly to repair the broken masts. The Top Gallant had already been repaired and men were aloft re-rigging the yards. The sound of hammer on wood made William feel as if he should be there with them but he knew that he was in no condition to do so. He watched as men, as black as coal with wide eyes and even wider smiles, carried sacks of provisions on board. Their skin glistened like polished ebony as they sweated in the heat. William had seen the occasional black face before in some of the larger towns back home but to see so many of them in one place was bewildering. The grizzled face of George Murphy appeared before him.

"Now boy, good to see you up and around. Here!" and he thrust a bowl of food towards him, "You deserve this I reckon." He nodded and went on his way. William sniffed the bowl cautiously, feeling suddenly very hungry.

"What is it?"

"Some sort of decent food!!" Jacob laughed, "Not our usual pork and peas, that's for sure. Tuck in while you can, it's all fresh!"

Whilst Jacob and Emily looked on William savoured the fresh meat and vegetables that took him back to the meals that his mother had cooked for him at home. With eyes bigger than his stomach he could only manage half the bowl before feeling suddenly and alarmingly weak. Apologising, he put the bowl aside and asked to be taken back to the infirmary, where, with Emily watching over him, he slept soundly for the rest of day.

Over the next few days, with Emily and Jacob's help, little by little he grew stronger and his appetite returned. His shoulder still gave him a lot of pain but, in spite of the handicap of having only one useful arm, he became able to dress and wash himself again, much to Emily's concern and not a little dismay. John became his constant companion. His own leg was healing well and although he now walked with a slight limp he was more than ready to do the fetching and carrying for William wherever possible. As they were sitting together on deck John said unexpectedly,

"You know you are a true friend William?"

"And so are you" William replied.

"No, I mean that are a true friend. You were prepared to lay down your life for me that night. I'll never forget that William."

"Yes, well…."

"That night, I can't remember much," William sensed that John wanted to talk and said nothing. Until now John had barely mentioned the storm.

"That night…..we were on deck together in the storm. Waves were crashing over us, beasts were screaming in pain and fear. I remember Henry being……." his voice tailed off into silence. The two men sat silently together. William placed his good arm around John's shoulder.

"It's alright John, you can talk about it if needs must."

"The beasts were screaming but the men weren't." he continued. "I remember trying to free a dead cow and then suddenly I am being carried towards the rail. I don't know how…..I can't stop…All I can see is the blackness in front of me….and I remember thinking 'Is this it?' Is this what death is like?'….And then as the blackness was about to swallow me up I stop and am pulled backwards. I can't remember much else….except that I am aware you have your arms around me, holding my head in your coat as the water crashes over us. William, I only hope that I can be as true a friend to you one day."

William nodded quietly and looked out over Table Bay, which lay in the shadow of a strange flat topped mountain, poking through its shroud of mist. The air was full of strange and exotic sounds; the guttural voices of the native workers; the songs of the porters loading the ship and the cries of brightly coloured birds swooping overhead. The sun felt warm on his face and William, having shaken the hand of Death himself, felt that it was good to be alive.

CHAPTER 7

November– December 1829

The Gilmore had been at sea for three weeks since leaving Cape Town. Captain Geary was heading in a steady south westerly direction hoping to pick up the westerly trade winds that would carry them eastwards towards their destination. They had lain in Cape Town for a further two weeks whilst repairs were completed. Thomas Peel blustered about the ship; his anger growing visibly with every passing day spent idling in port. There were many heated exchanges between him and the Captain but Geary was resolute and would not give an inch until he was fully satisfied that his ship was seaworthy enough to sail onwards. Time had been lost, everyone knew that, none more so than Peel himself. His goal of reaching Swan River by the beginning of November had long disappeared and in order to limit his loss of time he urged the Captain to take the fastest route possible, even if that did mean sailing further south towards the ice fields.

Reprovisioned and rested, there had been an almost festive atmosphere as the ship sailed out of Table Bay. New pens had been constructed by the settlers and some extra livestock, mostly sheep, had been taken on board. Personal luggage had been brought up from the hold and the damp and mildewed belongings had been laid out to air in the warm sunshine. Those recovering from their injuries received during the storm had fared well in the fresh air. Whilst in port fresh fruit and vegetables had been available and all had eaten heartily. But the buoyant mood of the settlers on leaving the South African colony had once again lapsed into the daily monotony of shipboard life. The fresh food having been exhausted their meals now returned to the routine of beef on Tuesdays and Saturdays; pork on a Monday, Wednesday and Friday and preserved meat on a Thursday. Washdays once again became the highlight of each week!

As the ship picked up the westerly trade winds around 40° latitude the Captain began to steer an east south easterly course, towards the southern ice shelf. The air grew noticeably cooler and flurries of snow became more frequent. William was now obliged to wear his heavy coat at all times. His shoulder was healing well and, although still a little stiff and sore, he had regained some limited movement. Emily had insisted that his arm should remain strapped but he had shrugged off her fussing, complaining that his arm would never be right unless he kept exercising it. Reluctantly she had agreed and, accordingly, his arm was getting stronger each day.

Standing at the port rail one morning he was

aware that the sea seemed to have a strange heaviness to it. Although there was still quite a slashing breeze the wave tops did not break into spume and spray as usual; instead the sea had a heavy dull roll to it. William peered into the distance. He could no longer make out the horizon, cloud and sea became one. A ship's bell began to ring and orders shouted. Sailors clambered up the shrouds and sails were being taken in. John joined William at the rail.

"What's afoot?" he asked.

"We're taking in sail. There must be something ahead for us to need to slow down" replied William, pointing ahead. "Look, I think that could be a fog bank on the horizon"

As the sails were taken in the Gilmore lost headway quickly and the breeze seemed to die away to an eerie stillness. Like a silent shroud the fog rolled across the sea and enveloped the tiny ship in its cold embrace. William could barely make out either bow or stern from where they were standing.

"I've seen fogs along the river Severn before now but never one like this" he said, pulling his hat down further over his ears, "have you John?"

"Never" came the muffled reply from deep within John's coat. Settlers were appearing on deck, drawn out by the eerie silence and the tolling bell. Some began to pray, others just stood in awe. Peel emerged onto the Quarter Deck and looked up at the Captain standing silent above him on the Poop

Deck.

"Captain Geary. Why have we slowed?" he demanded irritably.

"Fog bank" replied Geary. "As I feared. We're sailing into dangerous waters near the southern ice field."

"How dangerous?"

"Dangerous enough at this time of year. Icebergs are the worst. Great floating masses of ice that can rip a ship to splinters." He peered into the murkiness and barked out some orders. Sailors ran and lined the forward rails, long boathooks in hand to fend off any iceberg. The ship's bell echoed in the still air as a warning to any other ships in the vicinity.

Jacob, Emily and the children joined William and John at the rail. All were well muffled against the cold but the icy dampness seemed to penetrate; with each breath the cold air seared the throat. Emily pulled her shawl closer around her head and shoulders and took William's arm.

"I'm scared William."

"'Tis only a fog Emily."

"No, I mean I'm really scared. Something bad. I feel it inside." William gave her arm a gentle squeeze.

"You've nothing to be frightened of Emily. You've got Jacob and John and all the others to take care of you."

"And you William?"

"And me, of course, Emily. Now, why don't you take the children below and keep them warm. This fog is no good to man nor beast."

Before she could reply a great shout went up from the sailors at the bow of the ship.

"Ice ahead!"

Those at the rails peered into the fog. The sea had grown thick and, through the rolling mist, thin ice could be seen floating on the surface, crunching gently against the wooden hull. Suddenly another cry went up.

"Iceberg off the port bow!"

Captain Geary responded immediately.

"Hard a starboard!"

The helmsman spun the wheel as slowly, ever so slowly, the Gilmore responded. Through the fog a huge shadow began to appear. The amorphous shape began to solidify into an enormous block of ice that towered over the settlers, almost as tall as the Gilmore itself. Some at the rail backed away in fear as the iceberg loomed above them. Like a mother bird Emily gathered the children to her as Jacob placed his arms around them all to protect them against this new terror.

As the Gilmore slowly swung to starboard the sailors on the port bow set their boathooks onto the glistening skin of the monster and leant with all their strength, aiding the ship on its course. The ice giant cracked and groaned in protest as it slipped along the port side. William stood in awe, oblivious to the danger, transfixed at the enormity and beauty of this natural, almost living thing. He could have reached out and touched the ice if he had wanted to but he felt that he would have disturbed this giant lumbering monster from its path. Never before had he seen such beauty; blues and greens reflected from deep within the heart of this beast, pulsating with a life of its own. William stole a look at John standing next to him and saw the same awe and wonder reflected in his eyes.

On the Quarter Deck Thomas Peel's eyes reflected only fear and loathing. As the iceberg towered above him he had shrunk away to the starboard rail. For him this was no thing of beauty but yet another obstacle thrown at him. He was not a particularly religious man but how many more obstacles would God place in his path? He let out a long breath that clung around his head. How long he had held his breath for he was not sure and he unclenched his white knuckled hands from the rail. "Are there more?" he shouted up to the Captain. "Who can tell? Until this fog lifts we must all be on our guard." Geary never once looked down at Peel but studied the blank wall of fog ahead. He had a growing feeling of disdain for this pompous, self obsessed venturer.

The iceberg receded into the fog as silently as it had appeared. On the Main Deck only the muttered prayers of the religious and the tolling of the bell broke the silence. William was suddenly aware that nobody had spoken during the entire incident. He looked at Jacob and Emily, still shielding their children, and for a brief moment envied their closeness. John broke the silence.

"Are you alright William?"

"Aye, are you?"

"Yes, that was unbelievable wasn't it? I never knew ice could grow as big as that."

"I've heard tell there are even bigger icebergs out there."

"Really?" gasped Emily with wide staring eyes.

"Aye, bigger and more dangerous. Sometimes ships founder on their unseen rocks below the water, like an off shore wreck."

"Then pray God we don't meet one of them" muttered Emily into her shawl.

"But it was so beautiful!" exclaimed William.

"But weren't you scared?" asked Emily from deep within the shawl.

"No" replied both John and William together, and they laughed, their laughter echoing through the fog and suddenly releasing the tension. Emily threw her arms around them.

"For a moment I thought…..no, I'm being stupid. Forgive me."

"What is there to forgive Emily? You feared for your family, that's only natural."

"No, William. I feared for you. I watched as you faced that…..thing. Your face showed no fear but I was afraid. Why?"

"Because you are a mother" said Jacob, standing at her side children in hand. "Now, let's get these below and warm before we all catch our death of cold" and he gently lead Emily away from William.

The fog rolled around the Gilmore for another two days. Neither the Captain nor crew slept, always at their stations ready to act should another iceberg appear. The ship made slow progress through the icy waters and below decks settlers tossed and turned, unable to sleep for the knocking of ice against the wooden hull and the constant tolling of the warning bell. Twice there had been alarms and all who could had turned out on deck only to find mysterious shadows drifting through the fog but always just far enough away not to threaten the ship. The cold and damp penetrated even the warmest coat, piercing flesh and bone like a keen whet knife. William's shoulder ached with the cold and breathing became painful. Speech was kept to the barest necessity to preserve warmth; old and young developed hacking coughs as they drew in the fog laden air. Throughout all of this Captain Geary stood motionless at his post, the collar of his heavy seaman's coat turned up against the weather. Standing with his hands behind his back, staring intently forwards William had thought that he had looked somewhat like pictures of Napoleon Bonaparte that he had seen in the newspapers back home. Peel, on the other hand, had remained in his cabin and had not been seen since their first encounter with the iceberg.

On the morning of the third day the fog rolled away and, much to everyone's relief, they found themselves in clear water. The air was still cold but the sky was clear and a watery sun gave a little warmth. A breeze picked up and sails were unfurled and the Gilmore at last began to make some headway. During the night a child had died of a fever and several other passengers were sickening. Surgeon Lyttleton had said that exposure to the cold and damp had brought on the fever and it was only to be expected with the weather that they had experienced. Jacob was not so sure, as he stood with William on the Main Deck after the funeral.

"The young and the old I could understand suffering from the cold but now even some of the fit and active are taking to their beds."

"Nobody in the single men's quarters is suffering, as far as I know." said William.

"It's only in the family quarters at present. I'm keeping a close eye on Jane at the moment. She has started with a cough, although there's no sign of any fever."

"If it stays as a cough she should be alright. It's probably only a cold she has from the damp."

"Maybe so but I'm still worried about her. Emily won't leave her for a moment. She's scared the fever will start and that we will lose her."

"What does the Doctor say?" asked William.

"Pah! Doctors! What can he say? He mixed up a

tincture and told Emily to give it to her three times a day. What's in it I want to know? I might well be poisoning my child for all I know."

"He fixed my shoulder" said William, raising his arm.

"Aye, well, he may be good at fixing bones and stitching skin. In any case, bones will heal themselves if strapped right. This fever is something he doesn't know about if you ask me."

A sudden rush of air and a cry from aloft of 'Sail off the port bow' broke their conversation and they looked out to sea just in time to see the flukes of an enormous whale disappear below the surface.

"What in God's name is that?" exclaimed Jacob.

"That is the proverbial leviathan Jacob, a whale, one of the biggest creatures known to man".

By now other passengers pressed to the rail to catch sight of the whale. As they watched, three whales broke surface simultaneously not one hundred yards from the port rail. Their shiny blue-black backs arched in perfect unison as they rose and then sank beneath the waves.

"Yonder's a Yank whaler I reckon by her flag" said one of the men nearby, pointing at the oncoming ship, "there's no other ship to be in this area in their right minds."

"Will the whales attack us?" asked John, appearing at his father's side.

"I've heard tell of them attacking whaling ships but only after they've been attacked themselves.

There's no reason for them to harm us" continued the man. As he spoke one of the whales suddenly rose up majestically into the air and slapped down hard on its side. The slap echoed across the open water and a huge plume of water sprayed around. The other two whales surfaced nearby and blew fountains of water and air from their blow holes. They lay on the surface, their small eyes seemingly inspecting the Gilmore.

"It's not us they have to worry about" said the man, nodding at the other ship. It had changed tack now and William could see two longboats being lowered. With sixteen oarsmen in each the two boats seemed to fly across the open water towards the whales. Standing tall in the prow of each boat stood the harpooner, his iron tipped harpoon at the ready. As the passengers on board the Gilmore watched spellbound, the two boats steered apart to pass on either side of the smallest of the three whales. The whales suddenly sensed the danger and arched their backs to dive but not before the first of the boats struck. Steered skilfully by its helmsman the boat almost rode up the back of the whale and the harpooner rose up high and drove his harpoon into the head of the whale, near its blow hole. Seconds later the second boat did the same. The animal thrashed and began to dive and the longboats were in danger of being swamped. The harpoon ropes were paid out as the whale tried to escape but with the two iron headed shafts buried into its blow hole it could not stay under for long and, surfacing again near the longboats, it blew a plume of blood, air and water into the sky. Blood continued to bubble from its blow hole as it lay on the surface, its baleful eyes watching the whalers. The whale was mortally wounded and although it made one or two attempts to dive it was now far too weak to do so. The whalers sat in their longboats patiently waiting. When the moment was right the lead harpooner leapt onto the dying whale and drove another shaft deep into its head, before leaping back aboard. With a final thrash of its tail the whale then remained still, its blood spreading across the waves in a widening red pool. Attaching more ropes to the dead whale the longboats headed back to the whaling ship.

"Look!" John pointed. The two other whales surfaced and watched as their companion was towed away. They circled once and then, with a final blow, they sank beneath the waves.

"Just saying their farewells" said the man, "just like we did this morning with that young babby."

Edward suddenly appeared on deck calling for his father.

"Pa! Pa! Come quick. Ma's got the fever!"

"What? There must be some mistake. It's Jane as has the fever not your Ma".

"No. Ma started coughing last night, didn't you notice? She just tried to hide it. Now she's down with the fever proper and taken to her bed."

A cold hand seized William's heart. He looked at Jacob and they both ran to the hatchway. William pulled up short.

"No, you must go Jacob. It's her husband and family she needs now. Just let me know how she does." Jacob nodded and placed a hand on William's shoulder.

"Aye, I will. Thanks William. Come on lads" and the three hurried below decks.

Three days was all that it had taken. Three days of inner torture whilst William paced the decks. Oblivious to the cold or the rolling of the ship he barely slept or ate. Although he had desperately wanted to see Emily he had not been allowed to. Surgeon Lyttleton had declared an emergency and Captain Geary had quarantined the infirmaries so that only those who tended their loved ones were allowed in and there they had to remain. In this way the Doctor hoped that this unknown sickness would not spread further throughout the ship. The Quarter Deck passengers and the single men's quarters remained untouched by the hand of death; it seemed mainly the family quarters where the sickness had struck. There was barely a family group on board that had not been affected. Each morning a sailor appeared and nailed to the main mast a list of those who had died during the night. Those untouched crowded around. The list was never long but all were known. A roped off area had been created on deck so that those as yet unaffected but quarantined could at least get some fresh air. Healthy passengers were forbidden to touch them or go near them. Messages were shouted back and forth and each morning William got a report from either John or Jacob on Emily's condition.

It had been that third morning, dawning cold and grey that the unthinkable had happened. William and others waited for the morning list, huddled in their heavy coats against the flurries of snow. The hatch to the quarantined area opened and haggard faces appeared, Jacob amongst them. Unexpected tears welled in William's eyes and a cold numbness spread across his chest as he looked at Jacob. He took half a step forwards but words were unnecessary; he saw the loss in Jacob's eyes and turned away to hide his tears. In a daze he watched as the sailor moved to the mast and pinned the morning's list to it. Like an automaton he mechanically moved forwards, unaware of anything else other than the fluttering piece of paper. His eyes scanned the short list of names and found the dreaded confirmation of what he already knew – 'Mrs Emily Thomas'. He turned to look for Jacob but he had already gone below. He stared out at the sea, a sudden feeling of repulsion and loathing for it. Was this to be Emily's fate; to be swallowed by the cold waves with no marker for her grave? How would the family fare now without her? How would Jacob manage with the little ones? What about me?

His mind in a whirl of questions he returned to his quarters and sat, shrouded in a blanket until at last he fell into a pain numbing sleep.

A hand shook him gently from his sleep. How long he had slept he did not know. George Murphy stood over him.

"Now then William, they'm holding the funerals of them as died last night" William stared blankly at him. "I thought as how you'd like to know, what with you.....well, you know."

William nodded his thanks and dragged himself out into the cold evening air. The world seemed strangely silent as he walked out on deck. The healthy stood in huddled groups, grey people in a grey world. Five canvass shrouded bodies were laid out on deck side by side, three larger and two smaller. Which was Emily William could not tell. It was strange that death should cloak these figures in anonymity when each had been so well known and loved. Jacob stood stony faced with his children gathered around him. Neither he nor John looked down at the bodies but stared out to sea, each lost in their own private grief. Not until Emily's name was read aloud and her body slid over the side of the ship did William feel anything at all. He watched as her body disappeared from sight and felt an inner pain of indescribable grief. He felt a hand on his shoulder.

"You alright boy?" It was Murphy; old, gruff George Murphy who offered him his sympathy.

William nodded, unable to speak and Murphy squeezed his shoulder gently in support. "Come on boy. Come with me, have a drop of grog. It'll warm you up a bit" and he lead William below.

It was exactly one week later that the quarantine order was lifted by the Captain. William had barely stirred from his bunk during this time. Captain Geary and Peel had called them all on deck to make the announcement that the fever had appeared to have burnt itself out and that there were now no restrictions on movement around the ship. William stared at the sea, unable to feel the relief he should. How many had already lost their lives on this voyage? What was it all for?

"How are you William?" He turned and found John standing beside him. Words stuck in his throat and he could not speak.

"It's alright William. I know. I understand." And the two stood silent together for a while, gazing out across the waves.

"Ma thought a lot of you, you know" said John finally, breaking the silence. William looked at him. "She said as much, just before she passed. It was peaceful, you know. No pain. She said 'Tell William I'm sorry. Tell him to take care of himself'. Those were her last words." He studied William carefully, trying to measure his reaction. Finally William spoke, flatly,

"I should have been there."

"Aye, as maybe, but you weren't allowed."

"I should have been able to say goodbye."

"She knew you couldn't be there. We all said it for you William."

"I.......how's your Pa doing?"

"He's bearing up considering. He's been there before but it's the little ones I'm worried about."

"What will he do now?"

"One of the single women is helping with little Emily and Jane, who's still recovering. Thomas and Edwin are old enough to understand and look after themselves."

"And what about you?"

"I'm alright. We'll manage somehow. Pa says I'm the man of the family now. I'll watch out for them. What about yourself?"

"Me?" William looked at the sea "I'll survive. We all will. You and me'll look out for each other, eh John?" John placed a hand on William's shoulder.

"That we will William. I still owe you a debt for saving my life, remember? Now, come with me and see the family. They all want to see you; they've missed you." He led William below and amidst hugs and tears they shared their grief and began the healing process.

Time passed slowly as November slipped into December. The Gilmore headed relentlessly east north east towards their goal. Although the wind remained fresh the air grew warmer and occasionally brightly coloured land birds were to be seen flying by. At last, early on the morning of the

15th of December a cry of 'Land Ho!' brought all passengers rushing out on deck. There, off the starboard bow, was a thin dark smudge on the horizon. In growing excitement they crowded the rails watching in anticipation as the smudge grew larger until a definite land mass could be seen. Peel appeared at the Quarter Deck rail and called out triumphantly to the crowd of settlers below, "There it is good people! Australia! Our new home!" and he gestured as if this was the biggest gift he could ever bestow on them. All below gave a spontaneous three hearty cheers for Mr Thomas Peel; Captain Geary and the Gilmore. William stood with John and Jacob and the family. He grasped first Jacob's hand and then John's.

"Finally, we've made it. There were times you know when I didn't think we ever would. When I think of what we've been through together." They stood with their arms around each other's shoulders, looking at the rapidly nearing coastline.

"We are a band of brothers!" cried John. "A band of brothers in a new land!" and for the first time in many weeks they laughed together.

The Gilmore rounded a headland and it became clear that this first piece of land they had seen was an island. Peel shouted from above. "That Gentlemen is Garden Island, the residence of Captain James Stirling, the Lieutenant Governor of the new colony. I am assured that he will be there to greet us when we come ashore."

The settlers watched as the coastline of Garden Island slipped by on the starboard side and another smaller island appeared off the port bow, Carnac Island. Sailors raced aloft and sails were taken in, slowing the Gilmore rapidly. At length, and with some consternation from the excited passengers, the ship slowed to a gentle halt as the anchors were released some two miles off the mainland. A murmur swelled through the crowd and all eyes turned to the Quarter Deck.

"Why have we anchored here?" demanded a voice. Captain Geary appeared alongside Peel. He placed his hands on the rail and looked down at the expectant upturned faces.

"We've voyaged a long way together and your safety has always been first and foremost in my mind. I ask you to be a little more patient. We have to anchor here in Gage's Roads because there is a sand bar across the mouth of the Swan River. Although Captain Stirling has made some preliminary soundings it is still uncertain as to where the clear channels are for shipping to pass through safely into Cockburn Sound. I haven't captained the Gilmore all this way to founder on a sand bar like the Marquis of Anglesea!" and he pointed to a wreck in the distance ahead. "So, I ask for your patience and we will get you all ashore by longboat as quickly as we possibly can. I can't say any fairer than that." A general murmur of assent went through the crowd as Geary continued,

"The first two longboats will carry single and other able bodied men. They will then establish a beach head and shelters whilst the boats ferry the other passengers ashore. When all passengers are ashore we will then off load equipment and baggage and finally the livestock."

Whilst he was addressing the passengers two longboats were already being lowered in readiness. William and other single men, John included, hurriedly grabbed their tool bags and sacks and made their way to the port rail where they clambered into the boats. John waved to his father as the sailors bent their backs to the oars and the boats pulled away from the ship.

"Don't worry Pa" he called out, "we'll have a good shelter built for you and the children by the time you come ashore!" and he laughed and clapped William on the back.

With a fresh north westerly breeze behind them the two longboats skipped across the waves towards the sand bar. A line of surf stretched before them and a sailor stood in the prow of each boat, looking for the tell tale sign of a break in the surf that would bring them to safety. With shouted exchanges between the man in the prow and the man on the tiller each boat rode the waves as they funnelled through the narrow channel into the calmer waters beyond. Heading for a line of sand dunes to the south of the river's mouth the boats soon beached in the shallows and William, and John

leapt joyfully into the water and waded ashore. John raced William onto the beach and looked back. William was standing at the water's edge his arms outstretched, almost in supplication. He tilted his head upwards and called out,
"Australia!"

CHAPTER 8

January – February 1830

Captain James Stirling was a patient man but this particular evening his patience was wearing thin. Since meeting Thomas Peel on that first evening on the fifteenth of December he had not been over impressed by Peel's bombastic manner; the man was becoming tiresome.

"I am afraid, Mr Peel, the matter is quite clear. As I explained to you, at some great length at our last meeting, your arrival in the Colony was six weeks beyond the agreed date."

"And as I explained to you Captain Stirling, that was through no fault of mine" objected Peel.

"We can apportion blame where we like Mr Peel but the terms laid out for you by Sir George Murray were patently clear. You were to arrive in the Colony by the first of November 1829 with no less than four hundred settlers. In fact you have failed on both counts Mr Peel and therefore, as explained, your entitlement to any land grant is now forfeit."

Peel puffed out his cheeks.

"But that is absolutely preposterous! I have arrived here in good faith, having endured all manner of hardships on the voyage, with a ship load of settlers, livestock and equipment. Yes, we may have arrived a short period beyond the given deadline but, as I have arrived, then surely I am entitled to some land?" Stirling sighed and drew a document from his desk.

"Mr Peel, allow me to read to you a communication that I received from Sir George Murray before your arrival, dated the twenty ninth of July 1829. I was disinclined to reveal the full content of the letter to you but now you have left me no other option.

London 29th July 1829

Captain James Stirling
Lieutenant Governor
The Swan River Colony

The Governor is not to put Mr Peel in the Council. If, as is probable, his party shall arrive too late for fulfilment of the conditions on which he received his grant, he will have no claim at all and even if he arrives in time, I cannot think that the impetuosity and indiscretion, to use no harsher words, which he has betrayed in his communications with this department, will render him an unsafe member of a body whose deliberations are likely to involve both general and individual interest of great and yearly importance.

Sir George Murray

I think you will agree Mr Peel that Sir George Murray has made His Majesty's Government's position very clear". He laid down the paper and fixed Peel with a steely glare. Peel blanched beneath his ruddy complexion.

"Then what has become of the land?"

"I exercised my authority, as vested in me by His Majesty's Government as Lieutenant Governor of this Colony, to arrange a general distribution of the land immediately after the given deadline."

"You have already distributed my land?"

"I had little alternative Mr Peel. We had no word of the Gilmore since your leaving Cape Town and when the deadline had passed without your arrival the land was forfeit. There are a number of settlers already in the Colony, as you are well aware, and they have been here for some months already and have helped to establish settlements both at Fremantle and Perth, which we have named as capital of our Colony. Under instructions from His Majesty's Government it would seem only correct for the forfeited land to be distributed amongst them."

"But that land is prime acreage, much of it with river frontage along the Swan and Canning rivers" Peel blustered, "that was MY land!"

"Your land, Mr Peel? I understand it to be His Majesty's land that was graciously offered to you, through the Office of his Government, upon the strict terms applied. You failed Mr Peel, you failed!"

"This matter will not rest!" thundered Peel, slamming his fist down hard on the desk. "This matter will not rest and I have a damned good mind sir to round up MY settlers and return with them to England. And I shall make it my business to make it publicly known that the Lieutenant Governor of this Colony did nothing to assist myself or my settlers upon arrival. Furthermore, I shall make it clear that by your actions you have rejected us, nay, cast us out of the Colony solely because of misfortunes met with during our voyage. How will that look sir, when I understand that you are begging the Government to send you such numbers of persons as to populate and expand the Colony for His Majesty!"

"Blackmail, Mr Peel, does not become a Gentleman! And I will not countenance it. May I remind you Mr Peel that I have shown you every courtesy and hospitality since your arrival? I have played host to you and your son here on Garden Island. I have furnished you with your own lodgings, albeit under canvass but that is a misfortune we all have to endure at present, and I shall continue to do so until such time as this matter can be resolved."

Peel deflated slightly in the face of authority.

"I am grateful for your hospitality Captain Stirling, please do not think otherwise, but I can see no resolution. Unless land can be found for myself and

my settlers I see no alternative but to return."
Stirling sighed again and drew another document
from the pile on his desk. On receipt of the letter
from London he had shrewdly foreseen that such a
situation might arise.

"Mr Peel, I am not ignorant of your difficulties,
especially those of your settlers, and I believe that I
am a reasonable man. Allow me to put to you an
alternative proposition. The Swan River Colony is
currently centred along the banks of the River
Swan, stretching from Fremantle at its mouth to
Perth some ten miles inland. Your original land
grant, now forfeit, would have enlarged the Colony
south of your settlement at Clarence, eastwards to
the Canning River and continuing along the banks
of the Swan north east of Perth. Here is my
proposal. My surveyor, General Sir Septimus Roe,
and his team have surveyed the coastline some forty
miles to the south and the inland territory adjoining
it. Should you be in agreement I strongly suggest
that you make a formal application to the
Government for a grant of 250,000 acres
encompassing the coastline south of what is now
Clarence as far as a point where the Murray River
joins the sea at an inlet, which we will now call Peel
Inlet, and eastwards from the coastline as far as the
Darling Scarp. This tract of land also encompasses
stretches of the Serpentine River and the Dardalup
tributaries. I will support this application should you
wish to proceed."

Peel sat in silence for a while, weighing up this new proposal. Stirling had played the trump card; Peel understood that Stirling knew very well that he was unable to carry out his threat of return to England. He was being offered a way out so that Stirling would not lose face but he would make him wait.

"And is this good land?" he asked eventually.

"It is passable good Mr Peel, with good husbandry. There are particularly fertile stretches along the banks of the rivers."

"I would wish to see a proper map of the proposed land drawn up before making a decision. May I think on this awhile?"

"Mr Peel, you may remain my guest here on Garden Island for as long as it takes you to reach a decision as to whether you wish to return to England or accept my generous proposal. Now, if you will forgive me, I have other more official business to attend to." He gestured to his desk and then sat, making it evidently clear that this matter was now closed. Peel rose from his chair and with a curt "Captain Stirling" and a brief nod he left. Stirling smiled to himself wryly; Peel would stay, for all his bluster. He drew the half completed January despatch to the Colonial Department that he had been working on before Peel had arrived that evening and put pen to paper.

It is without doubt that many if not all have been more or less disappointed on their arrival, either with the state of things here, or their own want of energy to surmount the difficulties pressing around them – not greater however than such as must necessarily be experienced in the beginning of every new colony; and, it may be added, far less severe than those which the American colonists had to encounter, or those who first established themselves on the opposite side of Australia.

He continued writing whilst thinking about Peel. He welcomed settlers to the new Colony but he had no desire to encourage slackers or those who desired immediate prosperity without effort. He concluded his report;

Many of the settlers who have come should never have left a safe and tranquil State of Life; if it be possible to discourage one set of people, and encourage another, I would earnestly request that , for a few years, the helpless and the inefficient may be kept from the settlement, whilst to the active, industrious and intelligent may be a confident assurance of a fair reward for their labours.

The heat was oppressive, even at this early hour of the day. William stirred in his makeshift cot and listened to the incessant buzz of insects and the sound of waves breaking on the shore. Several

117

weeks had passed since that morning in December when Thomas Peel had waded ashore, struggled up the sand dunes and loudly proclaimed,

"This will be the site of our new settlement in the Colony, which I hereby name Clarence in honour of the heir to the throne."

Nobody had been there to greet him; there was no pomp or ceremony, just a pompous little man addressing his raggle-taggle band of settlers. The newly named settlement of Clarence lay some miles south of Fremantle and the mouth of the Swan River, and even further from the settlement at Perth further up river. Peel had planted the Union flag on the crest of the dunes and William and John had clambered up and stood beside it surveying the wilderness before them. The dunes gave way to scrubland which stretched away to a line of grey blue trees shimmering in the heat. Beyond the trees a hazy line of mountains could be seen. So this was the Promised Land? There was little shelter to be had; little pasturage and only the distant line of trees would provide wood for building.

As other settlers had begun to arrive on the shore William and the other men set about making rough shelters for the women and the children. Stowed canvass tents were laid out on the beach to dry but many of them were so mildewed and rotten that they were unusable. Some good pieces of canvass were salvaged but had to be stitched together. Using what little resources they had the men constructed shelters out of old barrels, crates and any other spare wood brought ashore. The women and the elderly unpacked baggage and laid out their belongings to dry in the warm sunshine. Throughout all this industry Peel strutted amongst the settlers, giving needless advice where he thought fit.

"Ah, Gaze. Putting your skills to good use at last, eh?"

William looked up from his task. He and John were busy fashioning two rough sleeping cots for the children from an old cask. He wiped the sweat from his face.

"Aye" he grunted, "Find me some decent wood sir and I'll be able to do a decent job."

"We'll find wood enough for you soon. More wood than you can use I warrant you."

William looked at John but said nothing and bent to his work.

"We'll need wood for burning sir" said John.

"We'll need fires to keep the natives away at night and for cooking. And what about food sir? When can we expect fresh provisions?" Peel became flustered.

"Yes, yes, yes, all in good time young…..Thomas, isn't it? Good God man, you've only just arrived and you expect everything served to you on a plate! I shall speak with Captain Stirling and arrangements will be made."

"Whenever he shows up" muttered William under

his breath.

"You have something to say Gaze?" William stretched.

"Well sir, it's like this as I sees it and someone has to say it. You promised us a land of milk and honey; a place where we would have prime land to work; board and lodging and a decent wage. What have we got here? It's a barren land, sir; sun, sand and scrubland. There's no decent pasturage for the beasts, no wood for building and no fresh water to hand. On top of all that we have to build our own shelters, as tired and exhausted as we are, because the canvass tents that you supplied have rotted!"

By now William's voice was raised in anger. Men nearby paused in their work to listen to this confrontation. One or two edged nearer. Peel was reddening with anger.

"How dare you raise your voice to me Gaze! I have brought you all here safely and yet you dare to challenge me over a few trifling matters. I am your employer sir! Where is the respect? You are a rebel sir! A dangerous rebel and I can see I shall have to keep my eye on you!"

By now the men were gathered around him, muttering their support for William. He had been bold enough to say to Peel what many of them had been thinking. Peel, now feeling threatened, turned on them.

"I will overlook the gross indiscretion this time. The hour is getting late and we have had much to do today. I suggest that each of you gets on with his work before night falls" and he turned to go.

"And will you be joining us for supper this evening sir? We can offer you a nice bowl of watery soup and a comfy billet in this barrel here."

Peel turned to face this new voice. Frederick Lipscombe was now standing alongside William and he smiled a tooth cracked smile at Peel.

"It would be our pleasure sir" he continued. The men guffawed with laughter.

"You know damned well I shall be returning to join my son on board the Gilmore this evening."

William made as if to speak but John placed a warning hand on his arm and nodded in the direction of the sea. William turned and saw Captain Geary striding up the beach.

"Mr Peel, sir. How good to see you sharing your expertise with the men."

The men laughed loudly and Peel puffed himself up with anger.

"I......!" but before he could explode in rage the Captain continued,

"I have just received this message from the garrison on Garden Island" and he read from the paper. "His Excellency the Lieutenant Governor, Captain James Stirling, requests the pleasure of dining with Mr Peel and his son this evening at his residence. He also requests that Mr Peel and his son be his guests upon the island for the immediate future to facilitate planning arrangements for the new settlement. A

boat will be sent to the Gilmore this evening."
"Thank you Captain. I shall return on board the
Gilmore immediately to make arrangements." He
turned to the men. "And as I explained to Mr Gaze
here, I shall be consulting with the Governor
concerning the provisioning of the new settlement.
Good day gentlemen!" And with that he turned on
his heel and strutted down to the waiting longboat.

That all seemed so long ago now, thought
William as he emerged from his makeshift shelter
into the blue heat. He looked around at the random
collection of wood and canvass shelters that had
been hastily thrown together by the settlers. They
were small but reasonably weatherproof and
ventilated, which was important as the summer heat
began to grow in intensity. It was now the thirteenth
of February. William thought back to the frosty
Februaries he had known in Churchdown. How odd
it seemed to be experiencing such heat in this
upside down world where winter was summer;
Christmas Day was sweltering; birds were all the
colours of the rainbow and even the swans were
black.

Sickness had struck again, mainly dysentery
of which several had died. A lack of fresh fruit and
vegetables had also caused a few cases of scurvy,
again causing some deaths. A number of settlers
had developed eye complaints that caused swollen
and irritated eyelids that yielded a purulent sticky
yellow pus. William himself had suffered for a few

days but his mother's old remedy of bathing his eyes in cold tea had brought swift relief. A canvass sheet had been stretched between four posts to create a small hospital, erected a little distance from the main dwellings and here some of the sick and dying were cared for as best as possible. Others preferred to be nursed in their own shelters. The situation of the settlers had grown more desperate with each passing day. Decent food was in short supply and what there was for sale had to be bought from Peel's store and paid for in promissory notes issued in the name of Cooper and Levey. These notes were worthless outside of the settlement, as some settlers discovered to their cost when they walked the miles to Fremantle in search of provisions. Fresh water and timber had to be carried into the settlement from some distance across the scrubland and this brought new dangers. Venomous snakes and other strange biting insects inhabited this wilderness and a few settlers had received bites and stings that had caused at least one death. Added to this were the ever present natives or aboriginals as they were called. They did not threaten the settlement but observed at a distance, silently watching these strange newcomers to their land. Although there had been no hostility some of the settlers felt uneasy and requested of Peel that he arrange for a detachment of the 63rd Foot, now stationed in the new barracks at Perth, to be sent to Clarence. In the end two soldiers were sent to guard the settlement.

Faced with all these hardships it was with relief that a sail was sighted in Gage's Roads that morning. William joined the others running to the shoreline. Jacob and John joined him presently.

"What ship is that, can you tell?" asked Jacob.

"Can't say from this distance but she's flying a British flag whoever she is" replied William, squinting his eyes against the glare from the sea. The children joined them excitedly. Beneath their tanned and weathered faces there was the pallor of near starvation. Their clothes were little more than rags now and although Jacob was trying his best to keep the family together it was clear that he needed help.

"Maybe they've got food?" cried little Emily.

"And more beasts?" said Edwin. Jacob patted their heads patiently.

"We shall see."

Peel appeared, mounted on a horse given to him by Captain Stirling. He raised a telescope to his eye and studied the distant ship.

"It's the Hooghly!" he announced after a long moment. "Gentlemen, the Hooghly. And that means that at last our provisions have arrived from England!"

A ragged cheer rose from the watching settlers. Emily squeezed her father's hand and smiled up at him.

"Food Pa, food!"

As they watched, longboats could be seen pulling away from the ship. Following the same route as the Gilmore's boats had they passed through the sand bar and quickly gained the shore. Willing settlers waded into the shallows to secure the boats. A grey and weary group of new arrivals were helped onto the beach. Peel trotted amongst them and imperiously welcomed them, in the name of His Majesty King George, to the Swan River Colony and the settlement of Clarence.

The newcomers stared open mouthed at the ragged mob before them; unkempt women; weather beaten and bearded men; children in rags. They looked at the ramshackle collection of shelters along the tops of the sand dunes. This was not what they had expected; these people looked more like starvelings, their homes a little more than a shanty town.

Some one hundred or more passengers gathered on the shore, sorting out their baggage and belongings. They had clearly fared better than those of the Gilmore and they looked in a far healthier condition. Eventually a man in naval uniform pushed his way forward and addressed Peel.

"I take it sir that you are Mr Peel?" Peel doffed his hat in acknowledgement.

"I am indeed sir. And you are?"

"My name is Reeves, Captain of the Hooghly lying off shore. I request that you now guide my passengers to their lodgings so that they may store their belongings and seek refreshment."

John nudged William.

"This should be good! What will he say now?"

Peel looked in consternation about him. The new arrivals were already shouldering their bags in readiness.

"I believe sir you may be under a misapprehension" he said. "Clarence is but a poor settlement only newly founded. We arrived only a few weeks ago ourselves and, as yet, we have had little time to establish ourselves fully. We have faced hardship and deprivation through the lack of provisions. I am afraid sir there are no lodgings set aside for your passengers."

"But where are the women and children to sleep?"

"I am sure that these good citizens of Clarence" and he gestured widely behind him, "will open up their homes, as poor as they are, like good Christians. For those of you who are able we have a supply of timber and some canvass to spare so that you may construct your own temporary shelters. An area of land in the settlement has been set aside for you. Follow me!"

He turned his horse and pointed the straggling band of newcomers up the path through the sand dunes towards the scrubland on the edge of the settlement that was to be their new home. William stepped forward and took a bag from a woman's shoulder. She smiled at him gratefully. Others followed his example and soon the people of Clarence and the new arrivals were shaking hands and hugging each other as they shared their loads.

Peel and Reeves meanwhile were in earnest discussion down on the beach. Peel had dismounted from his horse and was clearly agitated, his arms gesticulating wildly. William could hear what they were saying, even from a distance.

"What do you mean, no provisions?" shouted Peel.

"Exactly as I say sir. We were furnished with no additional provisions for your settlement" replied Reeves, equally loud.

"But I was promised food provisions, livestock and further equipment."

"That's as maybe sir but I cannot be accountable for that."

"Mr Levey did not consult with you?"

"I have never met the gentleman sir."

"You have had no communication from him?"

"I'm not given to lying sir! If I say I have never met the gentleman sir, I have never met him! I know nothing of this Mr Levey."

"Then where are our provisions?"

The Captain raised his voice even further so that settlers and newcomers alike stopped what they were doing and looked towards the two quarrelling men.

"The only provisions we have on board Mr Peel are those that you see stacked over there on the beach. We have a few beasts yet to bring ashore but once they are on land my job is done! Now, unless you have anything further to say on the matter I am returning to my ship!" and with that he turned and strode through the shallows to a waiting boat. Peel bellowed after him.

"Then you have left us doomed sir, doomed!"

The Captain did not respond and Peel mounted his horse and spurred it up the dunes path, scattering settlers before him. He barked orders to all and sundry.

"You! You men over there. Bring those provisions from the beach below and get them stored under shelter." He gestured to an area of scrubland on the fringe of the settlement.

"Get a canvass shelter built over there and get them out of the sun." His eyes lighted on William and John who were helping to erect a shelter.

"You. Gaze! And your friend there. Organise a party of men and get those provisions out of the sun immediately" With that he urged his horse forwards and galloped off.

"Let him rot!" John spat on the ground. "I'm not doing his bidding like a common slave."

William stared after Peel.

"I know John, but if those provisions aren't moved they'll rot in this heat and then be of no use to anyone. God knows we've little enough to go round as it is without losing these." He turned to the others. "Who'll lend a hand?"

Thomas and Edwin stepped forwards straight away and some of the other new men joined them.

"Good lads. Right John. You get some men together and organise the building of a shelter. Take some canvass and wood and make a simple sun screen over there on that cleared patch of scrub. It's not the best place but it will do for now. I'll take these down to the beach and we'll start hauling the provisions up to you."

They toiled through the heat of the day, William and his gang began carrying crates, sacks and barrels from the beach through the settlement to where John and his gang and constructed the shelter. A wooden palisade was quickly set up around it to protect the stores from any wandering wildlife but also to protect them from any inquisitive aboriginals. The settlers at Clarence had heard, from the occasional contact they had with other settlers from the settlements at Fremantle and Perth, of thefts of provisions and equipment by some aboriginals. Over the last few days the aboriginals in the Clarence area had become bolder. They could often be seen now near the settlement; strange silent black people with bushy black hair. They stood or squatted for hours on end, just watching the settlers. They seemed to carry little in the way of possessions or clothing; both men and women wore simple bark loin cloths. Most of the men carried fearsome looking spears and many of the women carried babies on their hips. They always carried fire with them in the form of a fire stick and at night they built no shelters but made a fire and all slept around that. William, intrigued, often observed these blackfellows as much as they were observing him. Standing at the edge of the settlement he had once raised a hand in greeting but had received no acknowledgement. He didn't find them particularly threatening, although many of the settlers did, he knew. The presence of the two regular soldiers eased their worries slightly and it was with some relief that they were now sent to guard the new meagre provisions.

William had got used to the suddenness of the nightfall over the last few weeks. He sat outside his canvass shelter in front of a small fire, not because he was cold but because the smoke at least kept some of the incessant insects away. Jacob's shelter was a short distance away and he could see him sat outside, smoking his old clay pipe that had survived the voyage, with little Emily on his knee. William felt a sudden pity for him. Jacob had befriended Sarah Wise, one of the single women from the Gilmore. She helped care for the younger children and became his regular companion although, for the sake of propriety, she slept in her own shelter. It was clear that Jacob had been deeply affected by the loss of Emily. There was a deep sorrow in his eyes when you spoke to him. The boys had coped well and were always out and about but Jane had not fully recovered from her sickness. Poor diet and the harsh conditions made things hard for her. William found his mind wandering back over the last few months to his home in Churchdown. He missed the lush greenness of the Cotswolds, the birdsong, the smell of the countryside. He leant back against the tent pole and listened to the settlement beginning to settle into the night. Across the scrubland he could hear the nightly rhythmic chanting of the aboriginals and he drifted off into a world of greenness, with cool flowing water and a pretty face.

Crack! William jerked awake. A musket shot echoed through the darkness. How long he had been asleep he was not sure. Voices called out from the edge of the settlement and William picked up his axe and ran towards the sounds. Others were running too, shapes in the darkness, some towards the sounds, others away from them. William knew instinctively that something was wrong, something was different. The wind had veered. The wind that normally blew in from the sea had changed direction; it was now blowing from the land and with it came the smell of burning. He ran through the last few shelters to the sentry post near the food store. Stretched across the scrubland before him was a line of fire, flames leaping from bush to bush. Driven by the easterly wind the bushfire was being driven towards them, scrub bushes cracking and exploding as they ignited. Dark shapes could be seen leaping and dancing behind the flames as it advanced relentlessly towards them, consuming all in its path.

Crack! Another shot rang out as a soldier fired into the flames at the shapes beyond, believing they were being attacked. William knew immediately that the fire was a greater danger to them than the aboriginals. As the fire advanced the two red-coats looked at each other and ran. William called out to some men standing nearby.

"Quickly, you, round up all the women and children and lead them to the beach. You, get a group together and start moving these provisions, they will be the first thing to be fired. We can't lose them!"

A scream rang out and one of the men collapsed to the ground, writhing in agony. A spear had been launched from beyond the flames and had pierced his thigh. William watched as his fellows picked him up and ran with him through the settlement. John arrived breathlessly at William's side.

"What can I do William?"

"Run and get some men. Get spades, mattocks, anything you can use and bring them here as quickly as you can."

"Right" John sped off into the darkness. William took his axe and cut through the ropes of the nearest tents and dragged the canvass away from the fire. Others had now arrived on the scene and followed his example. Soon the line of shelters nearest the scrubland was being torn down.

"Drag all timber and canvass away as far as you can. We must stop the fire from entering the settlement" shouted William above the roar of the flames. John arrived with a group of men and women.

"John, we haven't got long. The fire is moving rapidly. We need to shovel sand and earth over that line of scrub there. The fire won't spread if it has nothing to feed on. Do your best John; it might buy us a little time to save the provisions."

By now the acrid smoke was stinging eyes and throats. Neckerchiefs were pulled over faces to protect the fire-fighters. The men, women and even some of the older children shovelled sand for all they were worth, whilst William and some of the others began hauling the crates and sacks that had only recently been set there.

Then fate played a cruel trick! A scrub bush exploded in a shower of parks and, borne on the freshening wind, the sparks sailed onto the canvass roof of the food store. Dried brittle in the sun the canvass caught fire instantly. Those inside threw down their burdens and ran for their lives. William yelled at John above the roar of the flames.

"John. John! Come back now! You can't do any more to stop the fire. We need your help here!"

Figures ran through the swirling smoke back into the settlement.

"William, we couldn't stop it" sobbed John, sucking in air.

"We need to save what we can" gasped William, "drag the timber and canvass away from the flames."

"But what about the store?"

"We've saved what we can, we can't go back there."

They looked at the food store, now fully ablaze. The wooden palisade thrown up to protect it was now a ring of fire.

"Come on John, retreat is all we can do and pray God for a miracle!"

The soot covered settlers, now as black as the aboriginals themselves, made their retreat pulling down shelters as they went and dragging timber and canvass with them. Down on the beach women, children and the elderly huddled together watching the increasing glow from beyond the dunes. And then a miracle did happen! The wind suddenly dropped and then veered north westerly, blowing once again from the sea. In the settlement the blackened fire-fighters watched as the line of flames suddenly seemed to pause in its tracks, spitting and hissing like a wild animal. In places the flames guttered and died. Lead by William and John the settlers of Clarence now advanced upon the receding fire, shovelling sand and earth over the dying flames.

By daybreak the fire was out and the horror of the night could be fully seen. The eastern quarter of the settlement, where most of the new arrivals had been placed, had been completely destroyed. The food store was nothing but a smoking pile. The settlers stood around silently, singly or in small

groups; red eyes staring from blackened faces. No lives had been lost in the fire, except for the man speared who had bled to death when left by his companions. Most of the belongings and equipment so recently brought ashore had been destroyed and the provisions had gone completely, save what they had managed to save. A woman's sob broke the silence and a man's voice called,
"Damned blackfellas!"
All eyes turned to the charred and smouldering scrubland. In the distance stood or squatted the group of aboriginals as if nothing had happened. They seemed not have moved since yesterday; just watching, silently.

CHAPTER 9

April 1830

William reined in his horse and slid from the saddle. The sun beat down relentlessly and it was still hot for early autumn and the promised rain had yet to arrive. The journey from Clarence to Fremantle was but a few miles but here, at the half-way point, nothing could be seen in any direction. The track followed the coast north before cutting across Woodman's Point and on to Fremantle. The glittering ocean stretched away to his left and the seemingly endless scrubland, that the settlers now called 'bush', stretched away inland to the distant blue hazed mountains. He didn't mind making the journey; in fact it was a welcome relief from the squalor that was now Clarence. When Thomas Peel had asked William to take an order to the newly opened store in Fremantle he had jumped at the chance, especially as Peel had allowed him use of one of the few precious horses in the settlement.

Clarence had not really recovered from the disastrous bushfire of five or six weeks ago. The settlers had raked through the debris of the fire for a few days afterwards, salvaging what they could but many of the new arrivals had lost everything they had. Peel had shown little sympathy for them. He had arrived from his enclave on Garden Island the following day to review the damage. He had walked around the burnt out quarter of Clarence holding a handkerchief to his nose against the acrid smoke still hanging in the still air. He made a few cursory enquiries as to the state of the livestock; what provisions had been saved and then, as an after thought, if anyone had been killed or injured before returning to his waiting boat. He seemed totally disinterested in the plight of the settlement. Indeed he had dismissed he entire situation with a curt; "Well, we must expect these things to happen."

What provisions that had been saved were now being rationed. Some settlers had attempted to supplement the rations with fish pulled from the Sound. Others experimented in hunting the strange looking wild animals called kangaroo that wandered around the bush. The flesh was not bad and at least gave them some fresh meat, a welcome relief from the preserved pork that was their staple diet. Fresh fruit and vegetables were still rarely eaten.

Peel's noticeable absence from the settlement and his inconsiderate attitude lead many of the men to openly criticising him and there was a growing feeling of revolt in the air. A few of the free settlers had already packed up what little belongings they had and set off on foot for Fremantle, believing that life in a more established place would be preferable to the cesspit of Clarence. The track to Fremantle was now trodden quite clear as it snaked through the bush. One morning a few weeks ago Jacob had appeared at William's shelter as he was busy planing some wood.

"I've come to tell you the news William."

"Aye?"

"I've been thinking long and hard now for some time about this. This settlement is doing nothing William. It's dying on its feet even before it has got started."

William looked up from his work and placed the plane to one side. He said nothing but nodded slowly in agreement. Clearly Jacob had something important to impart.

"There's nothing here for me and the children" continued Jacob, "so I've been thinking that maybe I should take them to Fremantle. I've heard tell that land is available there and Peel's certainly not distributing his land grant yet, if he actually has any!"

"I don't blame you for that Jacob. You're a free man. Peel can't hold you to staying here if you've a mind to go."

"Sarah had agreed to come with us" Jacob caught William's raised eyebrow, "to look after the children, of course" he added hurriedly.

"Of course" smiled William.

"John wants to stay here and make a go of it in Clarence. I tried to persuade him otherwise but he's almost a man now and he can choose for himself. I won't stop him."

"That's good of you Jacob. I'll keep a close eye on him for you."

"I know you will William. You're a good man. I just thought I ought to let you know my decision."

"I appreciate that Jacob. You are right. There's nothing here in Clarence but it's here I'm stuck until such time as my term of indenture is completed. You'll find it better for the children in Fremantle I'm sure. When do you leave?"

"Tomorrow"

"Then God speed you there"

"Thank you William. Thanks for all you have done for us. And don't forget if you are ever in Fremantle be sure to come and find us."

"I will that Jacob. I will" and he took Jacob's outstretched hand.

William tethered the horse to a nearby bush. He stretched and yawned. Today he felt good, he was his own master; for once he felt free. Yes, he had to deliver a message for Peel but he was looking forward to catching up with Jacob while in Fremantle. He stepped off the track and unbuckled his belt and eased down his ragged trousers. As he squatted to relieve himself he heard a faint rustle and looked up. There, directly in front of him, stood a small group of aboriginals. Where they had appeared from he did not know. He had seen nothing; heard nothing. Instinctively he reached for the musket he had placed on the ground next to him. The lead aboriginal followed the movement with his eyes and tightened the grip on his spear. William saw this and paused, knowing that by the time he could have taken up the musket, aimed and fired he would have been speared. He withdrew his hand from the musket and slowly stood, trousers round his ankles. The aboriginal gestured towards William's manhood with the butt of his spear, said something to his companion and they both laughed. The men turned to the women who also began laughing. William realised the absurdity of the situation and could not help but laugh himself. The air of tension between him and the aboriginals seemed to have been broken and he slowly bent and pulled up his trousers. As he rebuckled the belt he looked at the group. These were no tribal warriors he observed. There two men with several women and children following. Perhaps a family group or a hunting party? Two of the women carried cloth bundles out of which protruded roots and stems. The two men both carried fearsome looking spears and the younger of the two carried a dead grey kangaroo over his shoulder. All of them were naked except for the usual bark loincloth. William suddenly found himself envying their lack of clothes and their freedom.

Now that he appeared not to be a threat the aboriginals continued to chatter to each other and laugh, pointing every so often at William. The taller and older of the two men stepped forward.
"Kaya" he said.
William stood confused.
"Kaya" he said again, smiling and he turned and

140

gestured towards the rest of his group, "Moort".

William smiled and nodded, not understanding but sure that the group were being friendly towards him. They certainly did not appear to be frightened by him. The younger man threw the kangaroo to the ground and pointed at it.

"Yonga"

"Yon..ga?" William mimicked.

"Yonga kaya!" and the aboriginals laughed and clapped.

The younger man hopped around whilst the older man took his spear and mimed stalking and then killing the kangaroo.

"Yonga ngardanginy"

William realised that Yonga was their name for the animal the settlers knew as a kangaroo. He could only assume from the mime that ngardanginy meant hunting or killing. He attempted to repeat what he had heard, causing much laughter as he stumbled over the words.

The older man pushed the younger woman towards William. She cautiously approached him and, looking back at the others and saying something, she reached to touch his beard and hair. William's first reaction was to pull away but he stood still and allowed her to examine his unruly mop of hair. She fingered his coarse shirt and then plucked at his rough trousers.

"Djurlap" she said, smiling. William looked at her

confused. She was a pretty little thing he thought, even though she was an aboriginal. Her breasts were still quite pert and hadn't yet sagged to the dugs of the older women; she couldn't have been much more than sixteen years. He was conscious of her near naked body so near to him. He looked at the men and said;

"I'm sorry, I don't know what she means" They just smiled back and nodded

"Wonja"

"Djurlap" she said again. This time she took hold of her own loincloth. "Djurlap" and then she pointed at his trousers, "Djurlap". Realisation dawned in his mind. He took hold of his trousers and pointed at her loincloth.

"Djur....lap?" he repeated.

She nodded and laughed and rejoined the group. The two men had created a clear space in the earth and were busy lighting a small fire. The women opened up their bundles and took some flowering stems from one of them. The younger woman approached him again.

"Mirlen" she said, offering him a stem. He took it, not sure what to do with it. She looked at him, turned and said something to the others. She took another stem and broke it, placing the broken ends in her mouth and sucked noisily.

"Mirlen" she said again, gesturing that William should do as she did. "Mirlen kaya!"

Snapping the stem William placed the ends into his

mouth and sucked. A surprisingly sweet burst of liquid flowed across his dry tongue. He recoiled in surprised delight and sucked again greedily on the stem. She offered him another which he gratefully accepted and he reached for the leather water bottle dangling from the saddle of his patient horse. He took a swig and offered it to the young woman.

"Water"

She took it hesitantly. He made a drinking motion and wiped his mouth with the back of his hand.

"Water" he said again as she lifted the bottle to her lips and drank. She nodded.

"Kep"

"Yes, water….kep" William nodded and sucked on the broken stem.

"War…tur", she attempted the word and they both laughed.

By now the men had lit the fire and cut a leg from the kangaroo, deftly skinning it and placing it over the fire. Soon the aroma of roasting meat was making William's mouth water. One of the older women took a large root from her bundle and, using a nearby stone, cracked it open to reveal a glistening maggot-like grub the size of William's thumb. She offered it to him.

"Bardi"

William shook his head and grinning she picked up the grub and, still alive, dropped it into her mouth. The look of horror on his face made the aboriginals laugh and chatter. The older man gestured and beckoned him.

"Yanamarru nhurra", there was no mistaking what this meant. William approached the fire and was offered a piece of roasted kangaroo flesh.

"Thanks"

"Yonga dhatj kaya" the older man nodded as William ate.

"It's good" William said, "very good"

"Wonja", the younger woman patted the ground next to her and made space for him by the fire. Unable to squat as they did he sat cross legged as he was offered more pieces of meat and stems of the sweet honey like gum. Much to the aboriginals' obvious delight he was even persuaded to try a piece of one of the grubs, cooked on a piece of bark over the fire. It was not as bad as he had expected, having the consistency of a runny egg with a rather nutty taste. He made much of rolling his eyes and rubbing his stomach which made them laugh even more. For an hour or so he enjoyed the shared meal, given freely; two cultures meeting in friendship.

As soon as the food had all been eaten the group began to gather their belongings together and tossed sand over the fire to extinguish it. William stood, not knowing what to do but feeling that he ought to do something to repay their hospitality. The older man turned to William and nodded, "Kaya" he said and turned to go.

"Wait" cried William and he stepped to his horse and took a small hand axe from his saddle bag.

"Here, take it. I can always get another. Please" and he offered it to the man. The aboriginal looked at William for a moment and then stepped forward to take the axe. He weighed it in his hand and then nodded at William again.

"Kaya" and then he turned and lead his group away into the bush, as silently as they had appeared. William stood for a long while staring after them, as if in a trance. Had all this really happened or was it the heat causing him to hallucinate?

Turning to his horse he began preparing to move on when he sensed that he was being watched. Turning he saw the young woman standing a little distance from him; the rest of the group were nowhere to be seen. After a moment's hesitation she stepped towards him.

"Kaya" she said, smiling.

"Kaya" replied William. She took a small object from around her neck.

"Yonga kutj" she said, offering it to him. William took it, a small grey pouch made, he presumed from the colour, of the skin of a kangaroo. He placed it around his neck.

"Thank you" he smiled. "The skin of a kangaroo? I mean Yonga?"

"Yonga", she nodded and returned the smile. Then with a sudden movement that caught William off guard she stepped close to him and thrust her hand between his legs and squeezed gently, pointing to the skin pouch at his neck. "Yonga" she laughed and then ran off after the others.

William stood bemused for a moment. He didn't know what to think. He knew that these aboriginals had different ways to the settlers but there was being friendly – and being friendly! This certainly wouldn't have happened in Churchdown! He placed the soft skin bag around his neck and pulled himself into the saddle, reflecting on his first real encounter with the people of this strange land. He had always been told how barbaric these people were but they had made him welcome and shared their food with him. How could that be seen as barbaric? They ate fresh food, which was more than the settlers did in Clarence. They had no need of money; no reliance on a food store. They had the freedom to eat when they were hungry; drink when they were thirsty. They had no need of clothing; clothes only make you sweat and when you sweat, you stink. William was suddenly aware of his own stench. It was little wonder that the older women had wrinkled their noses when he came near. And why wear clothes anyway, he thought? We only wear clothes to cover our nakedness, as if we are ashamed. These aboriginals had no such thoughts; they were free from all the trappings of a 'civilised' society. In fact, their way of life has a lot to be said for it mused William, as he turned his horse towards Fremantle.

As he approached the settlement some hours later he could see several vessels moored off shore in Gage's Roads. Small lighters were ferrying goods and people from ships to shoreline, upon which a small tented settlement seemed to have grown. Beyond this on the sloping banks of the river William could see simple wooden buildings with the occasional stone one dotted around. Each building was set in its own narrow ribbon-like plot, with a small river frontage, that stretched back up the gently sloping bank. Some settlers had already built simple wooden palisade fences around their property and others had created brushwood fences to help keep in their livestock. Some had even begun to create small gardens. William looked down on the settlement of Fremantle; once you took your eyes beyond the tented shanty town and the flotsam and jetsam of the newly arrived, compared to Clarence this was a veritable paradise. Figures in the distance could be seen going about their business; there was an air of purpose and order to the scene.

He urged his horse down towards the settlement, following the hard beaten earth track that soon broadened out into a wider thoroughfare that lead into the township. He rode past simple single storey wooden buildings flanking the road, many with covered verandas. He pulled up and addressed a man leaning against a veranda post chewing a wad of tobacco.

"Could you tell me where I might find Lewis's store?" he asked. The man pointed up the roadway and spat onto the dusty track.

"'Bout two hundred yards yonder. You can't miss it. It's the only store we have!" and a laugh gurgled in his throat. "Where you from?"

"Clarence" replied William.

"That snake pit!" the man ejected another gobbet of tobacco juice into the dust. "I've heard tell it's dead down there?"

"It's tough" nodded William.

"You're better off here mate. Get out while you can."

"Only wish I could sir but I've got my indentures to serve first."

"You indentured to that Peel then, are you? He's a jackass mate. You won't hear anything good of him around here in Fremantle, I can tell you. He's a laughing stock!"

William tipped his hat and rode on, pulling up outside a low wooden building proudly displaying the sign 'Lewis Stores' over the doorway. He dismounted and tied the reins to the tethering rail outside. Brushing the trail dust from his clothes he stepped into the comparative coolness of the single room. Adjusting his eyes to the dimness of the interior he looked around. Before him was a long counter on which were stacked bolts of cloth. Around the room were ranged boxes, barrels and crates of all sizes. From the ceiling hung pots and pans; gun belts; powder horns and kitchen utensils of every description.

148

"Welcome to my Emporium" came a voice from the gloom, "and how may I help you good sir?" The man appeared behind the counter. William reached into his bag and drew out an envelope.

"I've been asked to give you this from Mr Thomas Peel of Clarence." The man took the envelope and opened it.

"Clarence you say?"

"Aye"

His eyes scanned the letter.

"I should be able to supply Mr Peel as requested. You'll be taking the goods with you?"

"I don't know what it is that Mr Peel has asked for." The man read aloud.

"A quantity of silver cutlery, and I quote here, as befits a man of my standing."

"Cutlery?" William gasped.

"As befits a man of my standing!" and the man laughed. "I will have this ready for you tomorrow morning, if that is suitable?"

"Er….yes. I was planning to return tonight but..."

"Tonight?"

"Aye, why do you ask?"

"Aren't you afraid of the natives?"

"No. I've found them very amenable people" replied William touching the skin pouch around his neck "In fact, very friendly."

"You can't trust them" continued the shopkeeper. "We get a few here in the settlement. They like the grog, I can tell you. Some of them even work with

the surveyors plotting the land upriver but I
wouldn't want to turn my back on one! Fierce
looking fellows some of them!"
"They're just living their lives, like you and me sir".
"No, young man, they are not like you and me!
They are filthy, immoral and unchristian-like
savages. What we need here are a few missionaries
to bring them into a civilised world!"
"Has there been any trouble here then?"
"Well…..that's as maybe" blustered the man, "but
there will be soon, mark my words, unless
something is done about them!"
William sensed that the time had come for him to
take his leave.
"I'm looking for a friend of mine, late out of
Clarence. His name is Jacob Thomas, perhaps you
know of him? He's an older man with a
younger….companion, if you understand me. He
has four children, two boys and two girls." The man
thought for a while.
"I think I know the man you talk about. If it's him
I'm thinking of then there's some new plots further
upriver, on the edge of the settlement, no more than
half a mile upstream."
"Well, I thank you for your time Mr Lewis and I'll
return in the morning to collect Mr Peel's goods."
He nodded to the man and stepped from the half
light of the shop interior out into the bright sunlight.
        Mounting his horse he headed upstream,
away from the 'centre' of the settlement. He passed

a group of aboriginals standing and squatting by the side of the road. He raised a hand in greeting.

"Kaya" he called out. The men looked at him in surprise.

"Kaya!" came the reply in unison. William smiled to himself. His encounter with the group on the trail had had some benefits then. He could at least communicate with these people, which was more than many settlers could do.

Jacob's plot was one of the last along the narrowing track. Edwin and Thomas were the first to see him as he approached. They stopped their work and ran to greet him, all but dragging him from his horse in their joy to see him again. They lead him to the low wooden building where Jacob was busy mending a chair in the kitchen. Sarah was busy bent over a cooking pot and the girls were watching their father.

"Look who we've found Pa!" cried the boys. All eyes turned to William. Emily and Jane squealed in delight and ran to hug him. Jacob took his hand.

"William! By God, it's good to see you. What brings you to Fremantle? Are you alone?"

"Aye"

"How's John?"

"He's well and sends his love to you, especially these ragamuffins!"

"But come on in out of the heat. A drink?" William nodded eagerly.

"Sarah, get the man a drink." The girls ran and

helped Sarah fill two beakers with ale from a flagon. William gratefully accepted the drink and in between gulps of the sweet tasting liquid he recounted to them his journey to Fremantle ending with his encounter with Mr Lewis.

"Aye, he's a good man at heart" said Jacob, "and he's been good to me and the children since we arrived here. But he's a devout God fearing man and there's none sings louder than him in church on a Sunday morning."

"You've got a church here?"

"Aye, a small one. Nothing like the one in Perth though!"

"What does that mean?"

"Well ours maybe a hut but at least it's made of wood! St James church in Perth is little more than a rush building with a thatched roof so I hear."

"Then at least Mr Lewis can sing in the dry when the rains come!"

"Oh yes, and pray loudly for the souls of these 'ungodly savages', as he calls them".

"But you've had no problems with them here Jacob?"

"No, not us. We see them sometimes along the river banks or sometimes even in the town but they've given us no trouble, have they children?"

"Someone had a sheep speared the other week" said Edwin.

"I know" nodded Jacob, "but understand this Edwin; to the aboriginals an animal is an animal. If they are hungry they kill and eat. They don't understand that you can kill one animal but not another; that this animal is wild but that one belongs to a person."

"But that's stealing!" cried Emily.

"Yes, you are right. But our laws are not their laws. Not yet, and we must be tolerant for a while until we understand each others' ways. Now William, you'll eat with us?"

The rough table was laid with simple wooden bowls and spoons, all self made by Jacob and the boys, and a pot of mutton stew was placed in the centre by Sarah. Much to the delight of the others William ate heartily. The conversation across the table was largely about the plight of the settlers in Clarence. William voiced his opinion that much of the trouble lay at the door of Thomas Peel. He was so seldom seen in Clarence and his intransigent attitude towards land distribution; payments, and in holding the monopoly over the sale of provisions was fermenting a feeling of resentment amongst free men and indentured alike. The conversation began to turn political and, as the children were beginning to yawn and lose interest, Jacob suggested that Sarah should put them to bed whilst he and William made a visit to the local inn.

"You have an inn?"

"Yes, the Stirling Hotel. One of the signs of a civilised society is that men must have a place to retire to at the end of the day to share a drink and

gentlemanly conversation" laughed Jacob.
"Whilst the women of this world look after the
children, wash the pots and clean up. Times will
change lads, times will change!" Sarah snorted in
reply.

The two friends walked side by side into the
settlement. It was dusk and lamps were beginning to
be lit. The night air was still and, in the half light,
Fremantle took on a tranquil and picturesque
appearance.

"But you're well then Jacob?" asked William.

"I won't say it's easy here but life is certainly better
than in Clarence."

"Sarah's good for you?"

"Aye, she is William. She's good and kind and the
children love her, as she does them."

"You'll marry?"

"I'll speak true William, we live as man and wife.
What needs a marriage ceremony? I'll wager almost
half of the married couples here in Fremantle are
not legally married!"

"As long as you have each other eh? And that can
only be goods for the children, having a mother
again?"

"It is William, it is. Jane has made good progress
since we've moved here. She's much healthier now.
And Emily and the boys seem settled."

"What about work? Will you farm your land?"

"Maybe a few sheep, they seem to do well here. The
soil's not the best for growing but good enough for

grazing. I need to get boundary fences in place first though; else the livestock will wander into the bush."

"And will that be enough to keep the family?"

"Maybe, maybe not. Who knows? But we've got to make a go of it; things have become so expensive to buy. Butter's now four shillings and sixpence a pound here and I've heard tell it's only ten pence back in England! Tea is the same price and sugar now three shillings and two pence. I've had another idea though. Boats are needed every day to transport goods and people to and from Perth upriver. I've heard from some in the settlement that boats can be hired for five guineas a day. Five guineas William! A man could grow rich on that. So, I'm thinking, if the boys and me can fashion a flat bottomed boat we won't have the problems the keeled boats have in getting stuck on the mud flats along the river. We'd make a fine living William!"

"Then good luck to you Jacob. I only wish I could be here to help you."

"They're crying out for skilled artisans like you. You could be earning eight shillings a day here as a skilled carpenter. That's eight of the King's shillings William, not the worthless bits of paper that Peel pays you with!"

The lights of the hotel appeared before them out of the darkness. Unlike the other buildings in the settlement this building had two storeys and was full of men. The air reeked of beer and smoke.

Jacob pulled a pipe from his pocket and added to the fug. Two mugs of ale appeared on a table in front of them and Jacob handed over a handful of coins.

"Seems strange to see people paying with actual real money!" said William.

"Don't you get paid none?" asked a man at his elbow.

"He's from Clarence" said Jacob by way of explanation.

"Ahh" the man nodded as if that was all that was needed. "Indentured?" he asked again.

"Aye" William nodded.

"Poor bastard! Being indentured to Peel and all. You've got rights you know". Jacob laughed.

"Don't get him started friend, he'll turn all political on you."

"No, I means it" continued the man, "he's got rights. Look, I was talking to this here ship's hand the other day. He was fresh out of New South Wales on a convict ship heading back to England. He was telling me these convicts have got the rights to lodgings, clothing and food. 'S true. And health care! The Government has it laid down. Well, damn me, if they convicts have rights then your indentured friend here should have some. If not, he's little more than a slave and he'd be better off a convict! Think on friend." And he downed his ale and staggered off into the crowd. William hunched moodily over his drink. This man was right; he was little more than a slave to Peel. Jacob stopped a passing seller and bought a sheet of paper from him. "Here you are William. We have our own newspaper now, the 'Fremantle Journal'. Here, take it. It might be a little out of date now but I think you'll find it interesting." William took the paper and glanced at it.

"Thanks" he mumbled. He was in no mood to read it now. The man's talk of rights had unsettled him. He had much to think about.

"Jacob, my good friend, do you mind if we retire to your home now? It's been a long day and it will be an equally long one tomorrow and I need to sleep. I need to think."

CHAPTER 10

May – July 1830

When the rains came they came with a vengeance. Battered by gale force north westerly's the rain rattled through the tiny shanty town of Clarence. Settlers huddled in their shelters against the ferocity of the storms and what had once been a dry and dusty landscape had now become a quagmire of wet cloying mud and sand. It clung to their boots as they ran through the rain; it trailed into their shelters until everything was a sea of mud.

William listened to the drumming of the rain on the wooden roof he had managed to construct for himself. His shelter had now taken on the look of a hut; he had replaced most of the canvass with scavenged and salvaged wood so that at least he was reasonably well protected against the storm. All outdoor work had had to be suspended for the time being and William had gone back to his favourite pastime, whittling. He was busy carving a wooden doll for little Emily; he would present it to her the next time he went to Fremantle.

It was now mid May, some three weeks since he had returned from Fremantle with his head full of thoughts about the rights of workers and conditions of service. Several of Peel's other indentured men had gathered in William's hut on his return to hear reports of Fremantle. He had told them all about the settlement; about how orderly it seemed compared to Clarence. He showed them the newspaper and had read it aloud for those who couldn't read and told them all that he had heard about the conditions and rights of the convicts in New South Wales. At this some of the men became agitated.

"Peel's nothing more than a damned slave master!" cried one, James Gardiner. "He gives us nothing and expects everything from us in return!"

"I've heard tell" said another, "that if you're a convict you're allowed to sell your skills for payment when you've done your given ten hours Government labour each day."

"That can't be true! It can't be!" exploded Fred Lipscombe, who had voyaged out on the Gilmore with William. "How can you be a convict and still get paid? It beggars belief!"

"It's right though" replied William. "Jacob was telling me the same. Let's say you're a carpenter, like me. You get transported to New South Wales or Van Diemen's Land and then you gets assigned to a free settler, or even an ex convict. You're forced to work for ten hours a day but then, if you've a mind to, you can sell any further time but it has to be paid for." There were gasps of astonishment from the others in the hut.

"Damned convicts live better than we do! We don't even get paid, not in proper money anyway."

"I know" continued William, "my promissory notes were worthless in Fremantle. I was laughed at when I told people how we were paid. If it hadn't been for Jacob's hospitality I'd have been as hungry there as I am here."

"Then it's 'bout time we did something" suggested Edward Boothman.

"But what can we do Ed?" asked Henry Brown. Some of the others nodded.

"We could confront Peel and air our grievances. He's obliged to listen out of common decency" offered William.

"Pah!" Fred spat on the floor. "Peel! How you going to see him then William? Nobody's seen sight of him since he sent you to Fremantle. He just sits over there on Garden Island and he don't come near us!"

"And why?" continued William, "Because he's scared of us. He knows he's in the wrong but he can't face us man to man. I wager if we petitioned Governor Stirling and laid out our grievances he'd listen to us."

"You mean go above Peel's head?"

"Why not? Peel don't listen to us. I know; I've tried that before. So why not go straight to the top man? What could we lose, eh? We have nothing to lose anyway!" The men nodded and laughed together at this, as the beginning of an idea was forming in William's mind.

  William lay on his cot as the wind buffeted

the hut. Since that meeting three weeks ago he had thought long and hard about what to do; about how exactly the petition should be worded. He thought back to all those political pamphlets he had read. The petition needed to be honest and straightforward to make their point; not wheedling and vengeful. He needed to state their case clearly and request that they be freed of their indentures so that they could perform an honest and industrious role in the new Colony. William nodded to himself; yes he liked those words. Lighting a stub of candle he drew paper and ink from his box and placing them on his rough wooden table he began to write.

Clarence
13th May 1830

His Excellency the Lieutenant Governor
Captain James Stirling

Your Excellency
We, the undersigned indentured men of Mr Thomas Peel beg leave of Your Excellency to hear this our petition.
On leaving our beloved mother country we were promised by Mr Peel and his agents certain conditions of our service for him. Viz. Shelter, Adequate Food, An honest day's Wage for an honest day's work.
We contest that the said Mr Peel has not met

with these conditions. Upon our arrival we have had to provide for our own shelter from whatever resources we can find. We have been given a poor and reduced diet which we have to purchase from Mr Peel's store and when we have received payment it has been in promissory notes that have no value whatsoever outside of Clarence.

We therefore humbly beg Your Excellency to be freed of our indentures so that we may freely perform an honest and industrious role in developing the Swan River Colony.

We remain your humble servants
William Gaze

He laid down the pen and read the letter through. Yes, that would do. All he needed now was to get the others to sign with him and then somehow get the paper to the Governor. He folded the letter carefully and addressed it and then wrapping it in a piece of oilcloth for protection he placed it firmly in an inside pocket. Pulling on his heavy coat and hat he pushed out into the afternoon gloom of the rain and wind in search of his companions. After an hour or so of trailing around the settlement he had managed to get five of the men who felt as brave and committed as he was to add their signatures to his. A few had backed down for fear of reprisals but six signatures was a good number, enough to make the petition worthwhile. Those signatures now read;

William Gaze   Frederick Lipscombe
Edward Boothman   James Gardiner
William Russell   Henry Rice Bond

As William had penned the letter so eloquently it had been suggested that he be their spokesman should the petition ever be heard in person. William secretly hoped that this would not be necessary but he reluctantly agreed, saying;
"One man has to stand for all and the needs of the many outweigh the needs of that one man."
          Returning to his hut, feeling somewhat flushed with the success of his plans, his attention was drawn by shouts from the shoreline. Pulling the brim of his hat firmly down over his eyes he headed into the still driving rain and ran down the path to the shore. Others followed him, drawn by the shouts. Through the gloom William could see boats being hauled towards the pounding surf; men toiling oblivious to the weather. John was already amongst them.
"Hey William! Lend a hand here will you? We need to get these launched!" William grabbed a trailing rope and hauled with the others.
"What's the emergency?" he shouted above the noise of the wind and waves.
"It's the Rockingham! She's moored out in the Sound off Garden Island but she's in
danger of breaking her ropes in the storm. If she does, she'll be driven onto the shore!"

"Are there many aboard?"

"Don't know but none of the passengers have been brought ashore yet. She only arrived today. We need to help get them off as soon as we can."

The boat they were hauling was suddenly lifted by the swell and William and John leapt aboard and grabbed an oar. Bending their backs to the oars the men on board the little boat heaved against the wind. The rain eased momentarily as they pulled away from the shore; the second boat following in their wake. Talking was now useless; all effort was needed to keep the boat on course, rising to each oncoming wave and then sliding down into its trough. Glancing over his shoulder as they crested a wave William could see the Rockingham ahead. All sails had been taken in but the ship was pitching and rolling alarmingly in the storm. By the time they reached the Rockingham other boats had put out from the island to take off the passengers. William's boat joined the others in the lee of the tall ship and its massive bulk gave them some respite from the howling wind. Men rested on their oars, gasping for breath and sucking in air.

"Why aren't they off loading?" gasped John. Several empty boats were now waiting to take off passengers. Angry voices could be heard shouting above them and William looked up.

"What can you see William?" called John.

"I can't rightly tell. I can hear Peel's voice above.

He's shouting something about all single men first. It sounds like he's arguing with the Captain!"
Rope ladders had been thrown from the ship's side and frightened faces peered over the ship's rail above them. Peel's figure appeared on the Quarter Deck above them.
"All single men; over the side now!" Men began to clamber over.
"As you were Mr Peel!" a naval uniformed figure joined him at the rail. "I am the Captain of this ship sir, and I will give the orders!"
"And these are MY settlers Captain and they follow MY orders!" thundered back Peel.
"I need all able bodied men to remain on this ship Mr Peel. If she breaks her ropes I will need strong arms; not women and children!" Men froze on the ladders, not knowing
whether they should continue down into the boats or clamber back on board.
"Damn you Captain! I need men in my settlement not corpses. The women and children can wait." He leant over the rail. "You men on the ladders, get a move on!" The men began to drop into the waiting boats.
"You sir are meddling in marine matters! Allow me to decide what course of action to take!"
"And you Captain are accountable to me! I chartered your ship and I pay your wages! You will do as I say!"
"I am accountable to no man but myself in a storm

sir! This is MY ship and I will say what happens on it or I'll have my satisfaction of any man that says otherwise, damn your eyes!" Peel disappeared from sight, leaving the Captain to thunder after him. "I will have my satisfaction of you sir! You dare walk away from me!"

Men continued to clamber down into the boats, cramming in as best they could. As each boat filled it pulled away from the Rockingham, heading towards the nearer shore of Garden Island. As he heaved on his oar William spotted Peel climbing down into one of the other boats. He called across to John and nodded at the ship.

"I see Peel's not staying on board then!" he shouted. "He's nothing but a coward, that man! I think he's just been challenged by the Captain."

"Then let's hope he gets a bullet between his eyes!"

At that moment a cry went up from a nearby boat. A huge wave had picked it up and tossed it aside like a child's plaything. Men thrashed in the water desperately trying to swim and wade to the nearby shore. There was little any of the others could do aboard their boats but to beach as quickly as possible. Men leapt out into the surf to help ashore those who had capsized. Soaked and battered they made their way to the shelter of some rocks below a low cliff. Above the sound of the wind came an audible 'Crack!' as the Rockingham slewed in the storm. Another 'Crack!' followed and it became clear that the mooring ropes had snapped. Sailors ran to the rails and began throwing out storm anchors but this did not stop the ship as it rode the waves steadily towards the far shore of the Sound. Figures could be seen leaping overboard; women; children; and sailors alike. Livestock was being driven into the sea in the hope that they would find their way ashore. The men on the beach rushed to the boats and put to sea again; others waded into the water to help as people began to emerge from the surf. For a frantic half an hour or more survivors were dragged or helped from the waves until all were assembled on the beach. Miraculously not one had perished. Families clung together and watched helplessly in the failing light as the Rockingham was driven towards the shore until, with a mighty rending of timbers; she foundered in the shallows and slowly listed to one side.

Peel emerged from the shadow of the cliff where he had been sheltering during all of this. "Well done you men! All are safe ashore thanks to you!" he called.

"Aye, and where were you when you were needed?" muttered a voice.

"I shall be making a full report of the incident to his Excellency. Your work will not go unrewarded!"

"What about our goods?" demanded one of the settlers from the Rockingham.

"We shall wait until daylight" replied Peel, "and then my men will ferry you across to the mainland

and we will salvage what we can."

"So what are we supposed to do now?"

"You will shelter here in the lee of this cliff until daybreak."

"But isn't there a settlement here on the island; somewhere we can at least get shelter and warmth?"

"And what about the children?" demanded a mother. Peel surveyed the sorry group of people before him.

"Madam, if I had shelter to offer you I would. But shelter for you there is none on the island. There is no settlement here; they are all on the mainland across the Sound. You must make do as best you can for one night. You are all safe; that is all that matters."

There was a mumbling of discontent amongst the settlers but as they had little alternative but to comply they huddled together for warmth amongst the rocks. William felt a rising burning anger inside of him.

"Pompous ass!" he muttered to John. "Who does he think he is, eh? God Almighty?

Would it hurt him to show some humanity and take the women and children and offer them some succour in his own shelter here? God alone knows he lives on this island like King Peel, for that is what I believe he wants to be, King of Swan River!"

John looked at his friend.

"William, I've never seen you with such anger."

"Aye, anger it is John. Anger at that man's lack of

humanity. Listen, I've here in my pocket a document that must get to the Governor." He drew from his inside pocket the oilcloth wrapped letter; for all that it had been through it was undamaged. "Will you take it for me John?"

"What document is that William?"

"It's a petition to the Governor, signed by myself and several other of Peel's indentured men. Someone has to make a stand John."

"What do you want me to do with it?"

"There's a small garrison on the island. You're a free man John; you can come and go as you please. Take it up to the garrison tonight and hand it to the garrison officer. Tell him it is an urgent matter that the Governor needs must attend to without delay."

"What about Peel? Aren't you going to tell him what you are doing?"

"No John, it's best he doesn't know. He would only make life very difficult for us."

He offered the letter to John. "It's survived this night John, that's a good omen. Will you take it?" John nodded and thrust the letter into his pocket and set out into the gathering darkness.

Dawn broke and the storm had abated. The wind was still a fresh north westerly but nothing like the previous day. Scattered amongst the rocks were groups of settlers; stiff and cold but still alive. Slowly they gathered themselves together looking lost and bewildered. Peel was nowhere to be seen. William could only presume that he had made

169

his way to his residence on the island under the cover of darkness. Across the Sound the once proud Rockingham now lay foundered, like a discarded shoe. The boats that had been pulled up on the beach were now made ready and William and the others began the long day's work of ferrying the survivors across to the mainland, where they could begin the long process of salvaging their belongings from the wreck.

Over the next few weeks the Colony braced itself against the ever present storms. Pulses of rain would sweep in from the sea and rake the settlements with hard stinging pellets, sending settlers hurrying for cover. Upstream, rivers had burst their banks and unprepared settlers found their homes flooded and their livestock washed away. For the newly arrived life was a misery. Camped out on the shore near the Rockingham they sheltered from the storms as best they could, their belongings lost and their livestock scattered in the bush.

Rumours abounded in Clarence about Thomas Peel. Some said that he had been killed in a duel with the Captain of the Rockingham; others said that he had simply run away in disgrace. Whatever the truth of the rumours, the fact was that Thomas Peel had not been seen since the evening of the wreck of the Rockingham.

As the weeks passed more and more settlers were drifting away from Clarence until it was largely made up of Peel's indentured men. Even John had decided to join his father and family in Fremantle. William was sad to see him go; he had been his constant companion since leaving England but he was pleased for the boy. There was no future for him in Clarence; no future for anyone.

By mid June the storms had begun to ease and the settlers of Clarence emerged from their shelters. The air was now cooler and fresher, much to their relief but the rains had left a sea of mud throughout the settlement. William was helping to clear the track that led past his hut. A red coated horseman picked his way through the settlement, stopping every so often to ask a question. Fingers pointed in William's direction, although he was unaware, head down busy working. He looked up as the rider reined in his horse in front of him.

"William Gaze?" he asked. William paused and looked up at the stranger.

"Aye, that's me."

"I have here a correspondence for you from the Lieutenant Governor's Office in Perth."

The man reached into his saddlebag and produced a letter. "It is official business. I have been instructed to see that you open it."

"Is there a reply needed?" asked William, taking the offered document.

"I'm just the courier. I am not privy to the contents of the documents I deliver but I will wait while you read it." The man settled back into his saddle and

surveyed the scene around him with obvious
disdain. William turned his back on the man and
broke open the seal. Opening the letter with
trembling hands he read;

Office of the Lieutenant Governor
Perth
18th June 1830

William Gaze et al.
Clarence
His Excellency the Lieutenant
Governor thanks the above for their Petition
received the 20th May.
His Excellency duly commands that
Mr William Gaze and the other signatories to the
Petition present themselves at the Court House in
Fremantle on Wednesday the 14th July 1830 to
present their full Petition before G Leake Esq, T
Bannister Esq and J Hunt Esq, appointed
Magistrates of this Colony.

P. Brown
Colonial Secretary

William turned to the courier.
"I thank you sir for this. Would you inform His
Excellency's Secretary that William Gaze
has received the letter and that he and the others
concerned will be present as instructed."
The rider nodded and turned his horse away and set

off at a relieved trot through the settlement. William read the letter again, hardly daring believe that it was true. The petition had reached the Governor; he had instructed the case to be heard. They would have their day in Court to call Peel to account. He ran through the settlement seeking the others, asking them to meet in his hut without delay, and soon five eager faces waited for William to read the letter. There were grunts of amazement as he did so.

"So, we done it then?" asked Henry.

"This is out first big step forward" said William, "we must think of how we present ourselves in front of the Magistrates."

"Will Peel be there?"

"I've heard tell he's dead" said Frederick.

"I hope he will be there" said William, "He must be alive else there would be no hearing our petition would there? If he was dead we would be free of our indentures anyway." The men nodded and muttered.

"I heard it from a sailor off the Rockingham that he fought a duel with the Captain and got wounded in the hand."

"Is that so? And how does he know?"

"He overheard the Captain discussing it with one of his officers."

"That would explain why Peel hasn't shown himself these last few weeks" added Edward, "he's in disgrace."

"Well, I hope to see him standing there in front of

me when we say our piece" said William. "I want to see his face when we tell how we have suffered."

"You'll speak for us then?" asked Frederick.

"Any one of you can speak as well as me."

"But you penned the letter; yours is the first signature. It's only right that you should speak our claim." William paused and looked at the silent faces before him.

"Is this what you all agree?" The men nodded their agreement. "Then so be it. I will stand for us all before the Magistrates and look Peel in the eye. Freedom, here we come boys!"

The intervening weeks sped by. William found himself wavering between eager anticipation and uncertain fear. He was not frightened of appearing before magistrates; he was not frightened of Peel but, sometimes, he was frightened of making a fool of himself. What if I let the others down? He confided as much to Jacob on a visit to Fremantle a week before the hearing.

"What do you have to lose?" asked Jacob. "A man has the right to speak for himself and others if asked."

"I know" replied William, "but what if I don't say it right? What if I sound like a whiner just seeking revenge?"

"That you will never be! I've seen you stand up to Peel before! Remember on the Gilmore after you had been injured? You were not lost for words then and neither will you be next week."

174

"You'll support me Jacob?"

"Is it an open hearing?"

"I believe so. Any settler has the right to observe a hearing in the Court House unless the Court dictates otherwise."

"Then we'll be there, John and I. Would we let our good friend down after all we've been through together?"

The morning of the fourteenth of July dawned cool and grey. William and the others had journeyed over to Fremantle the previous day as Jacob had offered to accommodate them in his newly extended cabin, albeit with blankets on the wooden floor but, as Henry had joked, this was a luxury after Clarence! The six presented themselves, as well turned out as they could, at the Court House, a simple stone building with a plain wooden interior. Peel was already in place when they entered, his right hand heavily bandaged witness to the rumour of his duelling exploits. He glared at William as they entered but William gave him no acknowledgement. They took their seats on a bench on the opposite wall to Peel. In seats at the back of the room sat John and Jacob and a few other interested settlers. A member of the Fremantle Journal sat on a front bench, pen in hand. At the appointed hour the three Magistrates entered and took their places at a long table set on a low raised dais. The room smelt of newly polished wood and every sound echoed off the bare wooden floor. The lead magistrate Justice Leake, flanked by his two companions, coughed and began the proceedings.

"This Court is now in session and we will begin with the petition of Gaze, Lipscombe, Boothman, Gardiner, Russell and Rice Bond against Thomas Peel Esquire, their employer. Are these people present?" He looked up, the six men nodded and Peel responded with a loud "Yes, your Honour."

"You are all aware that anything that you now say will be on oath?" Peel and William nodded their assent. Leake turned to the men.

"You have a spokesman?" William stood.

"Yes sir, William Gaze. I speak for these men and myself."

"He is nothing but an agitator!" shouted Peel across the room. The Magistrates looked at him coldly.

"Mr Peel, you will remain silent until you are asked to speak, I remind you that you do not best serve your position by such outbursts. Do I make myself clear?"

"Yes your Honour" mumbled Peel sheepishly as he sat again.

"Mr Gaze, I will read your petition to the Court", continued Justice Leake. He read aloud the petition that William had written and then asked;

"Is this your petition?"

"Yes sir" replied William.

"And these are the six signatures of you present here?" He offered the paper to William who took it and showed it to the others. They nodded.

"Yes sir, they are." William handed it back.

"Very well. Mr Gaze before we continue might I ask if you have had any legal training?"

"Sir?"

"Have you been trained in law sir?"

"No, your Honour"

"The petition is well worded. It gave the impression that you had received some training."

"No sir, only that I have read much."

"Damned political pamphlets I wager!" shouted Peel from across the room.

"Mr Peel, I have given you fair warning. If you continue in this manner I will order you removed from this Court. Now be silent sir!"

"I beg your pardon your Honour"

"Very well. Mr Gaze, we are not unmindful of the conditions that some of the settlers have had to face over the last year. We have perused your petition but perhaps you would elaborate further as to why you felt the need to petition His Excellency, the Lieutenant Governor of the Colony, rather than take up the matter with your employer Mr Peel?"

William suddenly felt very alone as he stood before the Bench and he felt all eyes upon him. He paused for a moment and turned, catching Jacob's eye. Jacob nodded encouragement and a whispered "Go on William, tell him" came from Edward behind him. He turned to the Magistrates and cleared his throat.

"Gentlemen, Your Honours, if Mr Peel had been

approachable as an employer we would have spoken to him."

"By that you mean that Mr Peel has been indifferent to your requests?"

"By that your Honour I mean that Mr Peel has so rarely been seen in Clarence that we have been personally unable to speak to him."

"Ah…." Leake turned to Peel, "and what have you to say to that Mr Peel?" Peel leapt to his feet.

"Your Honours, since I have employed these men they have caused me little but trouble, especially that man Gaze sir! Since I first came across him I have formed the opinion that he is a dangerous radical thinker, a political agitator and not to be trusted! He even consorts with the natives!" William's hand went to the skin pouch around his neck.

"Mr Peel, the Court is not interested in your opinion of these men but would welcome your response to the allegation that you have been rarely seen in Clarence."

"Your Honour, I have much to do in the administration of the settlement, the planning of work and development, the arranging of goods and provisions. I have not the time to be constantly present in the settlement."

The magistrate turned to William.

"Mr Gaze?"

"Sirs, the fact of the matter is that Mr Peel has set up residence on Garden Island since the time of our arrival on these shores. By his very absence from his people he has shown that he is indifferent to our condition and not prepared to share our hardships."

"Absolute balderdash!" exclaimed Peel. "I have suffered no less than you men. I have weathered the same storms, eaten the same provisions as you. As for residing on Garden Island, doesn't the administrator of a settlement deserve a decent residence?"

The three magistrates looked at each other.

"Mr Peel. May I remind you that you do not administrate the settlement. Clarence is a part, albeit a very small part, of the Crown Colony of Swan River and it is His Excellency the Lieutenant Governor Stirling who administrates it. You are as accountable to him as these men are to you! Do not presume to go above your station sir! Mr Gaze, you may continue."

"It is a fact sir that before we signed our indenture papers we were promised a more than generous weekly wage, board and lodging and the promise of land when our indentures are completed. We have seen little of these promises since we arrived, if at all."

"Has Mr Peel not paid you then?"

"What payments we have received have been in promissory notes that can only be used in Mr Peel's store. These notes are worthless outside of Clarence." He reached into his pocket and took out some notes. "If the Bench would allow me sir?" and he offered the notes to the magistrates. They passed them one to another and scrutinised them.

"Mr Peel?"

"Your Honours, when I first arrived in the Colony I had little in the way of disposable coinage. The voyage had cost me dear, especially after we had put into Cape Town after a disastrous storm. Repairs had to be made and extra provisions purchased. The issue of these promissory notes was intended only as an interim measure to alleviate the shortage of coinage."

"Then you will redeem these notes for their monetary value?"

"That is my intention your Honour."

"And can you redeem these notes?"

"When I have sufficient coinage sir"

"Mr Peel, you misunderstand me. Are you in a position to redeem these notes?"

"I cannot sir, at present. I have no funds available"

The magistrate coughed and drew a piece of paper towards him.

"And yet I believe you have funds enough to purchase, and I quote here, 'a quantity of cutlery as befits a man of my standing'?" A ripple of laughter spread throughout the room and even one of the magistrates suppressed a smile. Peel flushed with anger.

"Sir, I have not travelled such a distance to Swan River to shake off the trappings of a civilised society!"

"Mr Peel, do you therefore suggest that we live in an uncivilised society here?"

"No your Honour, I simply wished to point out that if I were to live as my employees then I would be no better than they are. They need something to look up to, to aspire to." Leake raised his eyebrows and turned to William.

"Mr Gaze, are you thus inspired?"

Another burst of laughter came from the onlookers.

"Sir, all men are created equal in the eyes of God" William replied. A murmur echoed around the room.

"Radical claptrap! He would have you, sir, eat from the same plate as the natives!" exploded Peel. Leake raised a hand to silence him.

"Continue Mr Gaze if you will?"

"Your Honours, we are plain and simple craftsmen. We left our homes and families in England because many of us were on hard times, some of us even on Poor Relief. In return for our labour we were offered an opportunity to better ourselves in a new land. We knew it would not be easy; we expected hardships along the way but not like we have been served sirs. Your Honour, I am a carpenter by trade. My tools are beginning to wear and rust in this climate. I cannot buy new tools because I have no money to do so and Mr Peel will not replace them. How can I offer my labour; how can we offer our labour in such conditions? All we ask is that we be allowed to work honestly towards the building of this Colony for just returns. Without those just returns we are little better than convicts in New South Wales or in Van Diemen's Land; and they have a Government agreed right of shelter, clothing, provisions and even health care. Your Honour, we regret that we have been driven to taking this action but we now request that we be freed of our indentures to Mr Peel in order that we may play a free and industrious role in the future development of His Majesty's Colony of Swan River." In the audience heads nodded in approval. Justice Leake sat back in his chair and placed the tips of his fingers together and studied William for what seemed a long time. A hushed and pregnant silence descended on the room. Eventually he spoke.

"Mr Gaze, you have presented your case well. Mr Peel, is there anything further you wish to add before we retire?" Slowly and painfully Peel rose to his feet.

"Your Honours, I am not a well man. I am suffering painfully from a riding accident" he gestured to his right hand; a loud guffaw of laughter echoes around the room.

"Silence!" barked Leake. "Proceed Mr Peel."

"I have brought my settlers safely to this land. I have endured the same hardships on board the Gilmore as Gaze and Lipscombe over there. Through no fault of my own my land grant was forfeit due to the late arrival of the Gilmore and I have been offered poor quality land as alternative.

Provisions promised to me from England have failed to arrive. My funds are now in short supply and I live in comparative destitution. I am caught in a trap sirs, not of my own making. I have insufficient funds to invest in my land and I cannot recoup any revenue from that land until I can invest in it." With that he sat wearily in his seat, a deflated and wrinkled balloon of a man.

"Thank you Mr Peel. We shall now retire to reach our decision." The Court stood and the three magistrates filed out. William was suddenly aware that he was sweating profusely and he sat, trembling. Hands clapped him on the shoulder.

"Well done William"

"Well said"

"That showed Peel for what he is"

William sat, drained of all emotion. He looked across at Peel, who sat cradling his wounded hand, staring at the floor. He felt a sudden overwhelming pity for this man. He had lost everything in his venture. No matter what the outcome of the day was to be he would still have lost everything, whereas William and the others had everything to gain.

Time dragged slowly until the door of the anteroom opened and the magistrates filed back in. The Court respectfully rose and then settled in anticipation.

"Mr Gaze, I have one further question to you before we pronounce our decision in this matter."

"Sir?"

"It has been alleged by Mr Peel that you consort with the natives. Is this true?"

"I have no quarrel with the peoples of this land sir"

"But do you consort with them?"

"I have shared food with them sir and I know one or two of their words"

"I observe that you wear an aboriginal pouch around your neck. Some might consider this inappropriate and cause for incite". Peel nodded and made to speak but Justice Leake shot him a warning glance.

"Sir" continued William, "this pouch was given to me in the spirit of friendship; a friendship that I hope I have returned. I choose to wear it as a sign of that friendship; to show to our aboriginal companions in this land that we should all be friends. To ignore them, as I have witnessed some do; to treat them as lesser men than we is an insult to their community. Surely to exchange a greeting in the street is the sign of a civilised man?"

"You agree with the Lieutenant Governor then that we should embrace the aboriginal?"

"As a fellow man yes, your Honour. We must, else we run the danger of generations of discontent in this land." Justice Leake nodded and gave William a studied look

"Mr Gaze, you speak eloquently well for a humble carpenter" He placed the tips of his fingers together again and studied the paper in front of him.

"Very well. Mr Gaze, Mr Peel, you will both

stand." They did so.

"We have read the petition set before us by Mr Gaze on behalf of himself and the other plaintiffs and we have listened to the arguments on both sides. Correspondingly, after deliberation we make the following ruling to be set down in writing" He raised a piece of paper and read aloud to the Court;

Fremantle July 14th 1830

We the undersigned Magistrates of the Colony of Western Australia having heard this day on oath the statement of the six men named in the margin on the subject of the non performance of the Arrangements agreed by Thomas Peel Esq and his agents authorised to act in his name before us and other magistrates assembled here on Wednesday the fourteenth day of July for the payment of certain wages due to them give it as our opinion that under these statement, that Agreement has not been kept on the part of the said Thomas Peel Esq and we do therefore release the six men named in the margin from the service of the said Thomas Peel Esq and they are hereby simply released.

He passed the paper to each of the Magistrates and they appended their names;

G.Leake
Thomas Bannister
J S Henty

He turned to William and the others.
"You will each receive a copy of this document.
You are now no longer indentured men; you are
free settlers of the Colony of Swan River.
Congratulations!"
There was a moment of stunned silence before a
roar of cheering and clapping rose from the Court.
Men clapped each other on the back and shook
hands as Peel slunk away through the crowd.
William sat motionless. John and Jacob ran to him.
"You've done it William, you've won! You're a
free man now!"

CHAPTER 11

June 1832

William settled back in his chair and watched John playing with the dog. It had been almost two years since he had gained his freedom from Peel and here he was now, sitting on his own veranda, outside of his own cabin, on his own land. Admittedly the land still had much clearing to be done but it was his; a plot of land running up from the south bank of the Canning River to the track known as River Road leading into the small settlement of Kelmscott.

He took a sip from the mug in his hand and thought back over the last two years. Within two weeks of being freed from his indentures he had packed up his few belongings in Clarence and moved to Fremantle. Jacob had offered him a bed until such time as he could get on his own feet and so William and the Thomas family were reunited, much to everyone's happiness. On the second day in Fremantle William had found work, carpentry skills being in great demand as the settlement developed and expanded. Now with money in his pocket instead of those worthless promissory notes he felt a new purpose in life. He was no longer at the beck and call of a master; he was a free man; his own master. Now he need not feel guilty about taking Jacob's hospitality as he could contribute towards the family's living costs each week. Jacob himself was doing well. He had followed through with his boat idea and had constructed not one but two flat bottomed boats and he had been plying his ferrying trade between Fremantle and Perth and beyond to the newer settlements upriver. Depending on the length of the journey and the nature of the goods being carried he could easily command a five guinea charge. With two boats in operation and John and the boys helping him it was proving to be a lucrative business.

In part payment for his board and lodging William had erected boundary fences around Jacob's property and together they had also built a small barn, which Jacob then suggested that William should use a workshop. This was good as it gave William somewhere to store his growing collection of tools as well as somewhere to work on the smaller commissions he seemed to be getting a lot of. He soon established a reputation for himself as a skilled craftsman who would charge an honest fee for his time and efforts. It was not so long before larger projects had begun to roll in and he had spent many months recently working on the construction of a new inn for John Butler, on the Fremantle to Perth track. In fact he had so much work there he had moved his belongings out of Jacob's home and into Butler's new place. Already his fee stood at somewhere around forty pounds and the work had yet to be completed.

William leaned back and stretched his legs. Life was now good, he thought to himself; at long last he was feeling positive about having moved to Australia. As the settlements had spread outwards along the rivers from Fremantle and Perth so more land had become available. William had made an application for land and had been granted an unsurveyed plot of fifty acres fronting the Canning River about a mile or so outside of the small settlement of Kelmscott. The land was on the south bank of the river at a point where the river took a northwards bend. His first task had been to build himself a home and, with the help of Jacob and the boys, it had taken several months of felling timber to build the cabin he sat in now. He looked around at his work. It was a simple two roomed single storey building, clad in timber with a timber roof. Some of the other settlers had settled for rush roofs but William knew from bitter experience that this didn't always stand up to the winter rains. He had made sure that his cabin was raised off the ground on stone supports to stop the dreaded white ants from attacking the woodwork. A covered veranda running the length of the building, with steps down to the land facing the river completed the picture. It was simple but it was home.

The heavy work of clearing the land ready for planting had begun in earnest earlier in the year. William had no pretensions about being a farmer but he wanted to be able to support himself and what he didn't use could always be sold. Dividing his time between his carpentry work in the settlements and working on his land he found he had rarely any free time at all. John had offered to help with the clearing as the winter months were quieter on the river and William was grateful for that. With the two of them working together the work had progressed steadily. It was now the fourteenth of June and William hoped that they would clear enough land along the river frontage ready for spring sowing. His plan was to be able to move out to his land permanently by early next year and to set up his workshop here.

John flopped down on the veranda steps. "Damn dog tires me out!" The dog lolloped over to him dragging a small branch in its jaws. It was a dog of indeterminate parentage, perhaps even half dingo, the native dog of the area. It had found William rather than William taking it on. It had turned up one day and William had thrown it a few scraps and so it stayed. It was an agreeable arrangement; the dog had food and shelter and in return William had gained companionship and protection. Protection had become the watchword of the settlers as their lands spread out from the settlements along the river banks like ever expanding tentacles of urbanisation. Aboriginals were now frequent visitors to the settlements and were happy to accept food and clothing where offered but there had also been an increase in the incidents of theft being reported across the Colony. There had even been one report of aboriginal violence towards a settler in Melville earlier last year. William had never experienced any problems with the aboriginals and he always greeted them when he met them and was greeted in return; friendship breeds friendship he had always maintained. But settlers were now keeping dogs to raise the alarm should their property or persons be threatened and the carrying of firearms was now commonplace, especially in the remoter areas. William owned a gun, like others, but he usually kept it in the cabin. He knew where it was if it was ever needed. He threw the slops over the veranda and yawned.

"Come on then John. You can stop playing around with the dog there. We've got a lot of work to get through today."

"Alright then, what's the plan for this afternoon?"

"I reckon that if we can clear that last half an acre of bush down by the river we'll have done well today."

"Best get on then"

"Aye" William picked up his axe and, tying the dog to the veranda rail, and they set off down the slope to the river. A small fire was still smouldering where they had cleared in the morning and the smoke hung heavy in the autumn air. The two men set to work slashing and cutting back the low thick brush that covered the ground. It was warm work and even in the cool air they worked in their shirt sleeves. They spoke little; their efforts focused upon their work. Suddenly the frenzied barking of the dog drew their attention. They looked towards the cabin and saw an unusually large group of aboriginals watching them, some twenty in all estimated William. He raised a hand in greeting. "Kaya!" he called up to them. The greeting was not returned. William felt uneasy and out of the corner of his eye he saw John pick up his shovel. This group was unlike any other he had encountered before. They were all men and all of them were armed with the long vicious looking barbed spears. "Kaya!" he called again. The dog continued barking and one of the aboriginals, taller than any William had seen, stepped forward and drove his spear into the animal. The dog howled in pain as other aboriginals joined in a frenzied stabbing attack. Instinctively William and John stepped forwards; William clutching his axe and John his shovel. "Hey! You!" shouted William, "Leave the dog, you bastard!"

The aboriginals ignored him and continued the attack until the dog lay still and silent, its blood beginning to trickle down the veranda steps.

William made towards them again.

"What the hell do you think you're doing?" He felt a hand on his arm.

"William, come away" said John in a hushed tone.

"They're after blood, like as not us next. Come away!"

"Not until I know why they killed my dog!"

"William, there's two of us and many more of them. You've got an axe and me a shovel. They've all got spears. We haven't even got our muskets, they're in the cabin!" John pulled at William's arm but he shrugged him off, stepping forward again.

"Kaya!"

The tall aboriginal turned to look at the two men. He looked back at his companions and said something and they laughed and then turning he raised his spear and hurled it at William and John. They froze as it buried itself in the ground near them; too near! The aboriginals had made their intentions clear. William was the first to react.

"Quick John, the river!" We need to get across it." He grabbed John's arm and they ran headlong back down the slope towards the Canning. Spears rained down on them, the aboriginals in hot pursuit.

"John, make for the log. Get across it!"

The river was broad at this point in its bend but a fallen log made a rough bridge across it to a spit of silt in the slower water of the far bank. John, being the younger of the two, had run ahead and made for the log; his lighter skin boots making quick work of the slippery bridge. William, in his heavy workman's boots, lagged behind and by the time he reached the river John was across.

"Come on William, you can do it! Hurry!"

John watched in horror as William, balancing his way along the log slipped and fell heavily. The aboriginals were within throwing range again. Hauling himself out of the water William paused and glanced over his shoulder as a spear took him squarely in the back. He pitched forward and began to crawl. He looked up at John on the bank.

"Go boy, run! Run to the barracks"

"Come on William" John stepped forwards and reached out a hand but was driven back by spears falling around him.

"Go John, save yourself!"

John watched as he aboriginals surrounded William. The tall leader took a spear from an older man and drove it into the helpless William; others joining in. John turned and ran, trying to block out the screams of pain from behind him. Head down he ran as fast as he could until he was out of spear range; the spiny bush thorns tearing at his legs. He knew he had to get to the barracks at Kelmscott; the military were there; they would help. Tears coursed down his face and all he could see whilst he was running was the sight of William being speared like a dog; and he had been helpless to do anything.

He crashed through the door into the barracks. A soldier on duty looked up in surprise. "Hold hard lad, what's the rush eh?" John doubled over, sucking in air.

"Aboriginals……..spears…….William" he gasped.

"Aboriginals? Where?"

"'Bout a mile upriver"

"Say again, what's happened?"

"My friend….William…..has been speared by natives" John finally managed to blurt out.

"We need to help him"

"There's only me and another here, and he's lame! The rest of the detachment is with Governor Ellis in Perth today"

"Then let's go!" demanded John, "We have to help William. Now!"

Hastily grabbing their muskets the soldier and his lame companion followed John out. Much to John's frustration they made slow progress, because of the soldier's lameness and their own nervousness. As they finally approached the site the two soldiers started calling out to each other to try and give the impression that there were many more than just the two of them. John raised a hand and they fell silent. Creeping cautiously ahead John thought he could hear a faint moaning sound. Crawling on his belly through the bush he peered down into the river bed. The aboriginals were nowhere to be seen but William was lying face down in the mud, four of the long spears protruding from his body and another lying near his head.

"He's over here!" shouted John and slid down the banking towards William.

"Christ, William! What have they done to you?" A faint moan was all that William could reply; he was still unbelievably alive. John raised William's head from the mud and cleared the filth from his face. Blood bubbled from his mouth and his eyes flickered.

"John?" he barely wheezed

"Don't talk William. We'll get you out of here."
He looked down at William. Two spears were in his back, another had been driven into his ribs, a fourth protruded from his neck and a fifth had pierced his cheek but had fallen out onto the ground, leaving a large ragged wound. One of the soldiers vomited onto the ground.

"Jesus, is he still alive?" John nodded.

"We've got to get him out of here."

"How, with those things still in him? We can't carry him"

"You'll have to pull 'em out" said the vomiting soldier, dragging the back of his hand across his mouth.

"And have him bleed to death? These spears are barbed. If we pull them they'll rip his flesh apart"

"Then what can we do, eh? We can't stay here" The two soldiers were becoming edgy, constantly peering around and expecting to be attacked at any moment.

"We'll have to cut the shafts off at skin level. That way we can carry him back to the barracks" John bent over William. "Hold on there William, can you hear me?" A low moan escaped William's lips.

"Good, listen, I know this will hurt but it's all I can

do. I'm going to get a saw and take off these damn spears as near to your skin as possible. Then I'll carry you to Kelmscott myself and get a surgeon. Right?" William moaned again.

"Right, you two. You stay here and guard him and keep talking to him. I'm going to run up to the cabin and get a saw."

"What about them blackfellas?"

"Bugger the blackfellas! It's him is all I care about!"

John grabbed a musket and set off at a run up the slope towards the cabin. All was silent. He cautiously stepped over the body of the dead dog, its bulk now lying limply like a deflated balloon, a few late flies buzzing around the corpse. The door of the cabin was open and, holding the musket at the ready, he stepped into the room. It was empty except for overturned furniture and broken utensils lying around. The aboriginals had taken all the wheat and seed and anything else they could carry away, even the guns and ammunition. Checking the other room and now sure the aboriginals had definitely gone John rooted in William's tool bag until he found the small saw he was looking for and ran back to the waiting men. In the fading afternoon light of that wintery day it could have been the subject of an oil painting; two red coated soldiers kneeling at the side of a fallen comrade, but John had no time for sentimentality, he knew that speed was now of the essence. Throwing down the musket he bent over William.

"This is going to hurt William but I don't know what else to do!" The breath was rasping in William's throat. "Right, you two. You hold him in case he jerks in pain and you, hold the shaft of this spear firmly while I cut. Don't let it move in his body."

John bent to the task. Carefully and as quickly as he could without causing further damage to William's body he sawed through the shaft of each spear. With every saw stroke William moaned and blood bubbled from his mouth. Sweat covered John's brow as he worked; the two soldiers silent and watchful. Finally the last shaft was sawn through and John let out a long breath. He threw down the saw.

"Now, no delay. Help lift him onto my shoulders" Between them they painfully lifted William and set off towards Kelmscott, John carrying William across his shoulders like a shepherd with a lost sheep.

It was barely a mile to Kelmscott. John kept up a steady pace conscious of the need to get there quickly but also that every step he took must be causing William unimaginable pain. He could hear William's shallow breathing rattling in his throat and he could feel the warm blood from William's wounds trickling over his skin. By the time they reached Kelmscott lamps were being lit around the settlement. Entering the barracks John laid William on an empty cot and sank exhausted to his knees. The two soldiers followed him in.

"Well done lad. We'll send to Fremantle for the surgeon"

"You mean there's no doctor here in Kelmscott?" John asked in dismay.

"'Fraid not lad. It's only a small settlement here. I'll send a rider straight away. 'T'aint far to Fremantle. A matter of hours and the surgeon will be here for your friend" He turned to his companion and scratching a few words on a piece of paper gave him some instructions and he hobbled out.

Hours passed and John would not leave William's side. He bathed his face and pressed a damp cloth to William's lips every so often. He cut away William's shirt from around the stubs of the spear shafts; the wounds burned red and angry and blood still oozed from them. William faded in and out of consciousness and his breath came in rasping moans. Once or twice John thought he heard him trying to form words and he lowered his ear to William's lips to try and catch what he was saying but to no avail. Once, William had opened his eyes wide and cried out but then immediately had lapsed into unconsciousness again. Shortly after midnight the rattle of horses hooves were heard outside and a soldier entered with two other men.

"Good evening. I'm Mr Langley, surgeon at Fremantle. I'm assuming this is the patient?" The other man sat at the table. John nodded and pulled back the cover he had placed over William. The surgeon looked for what seemed a long time.

"Good God" he eventually said quietly. "How came this about?"

John explained as fully as he could as Langley examined each of the wounds.

"It's a miracle he is still alive my friend. I've seen a few spear wounds in my time but never as many as this in one man, and still alive"

"Can you do anything doctor?"

"Each spear head will have to be removed separately. That means four separate operations in succession. I don't know if he will survive the shock of all that. Even if he does I can't guarantee that infection won't set in."

"But he's a fit man doctor"

"So well and good. But I've seen many a man taken by one spear, let alone four!"

"But you'll try? You have to!"

"I'm a surgeon lad, and a damned good one! I will try but I will give you no guarantee. Now, has he a Will and Testament?"

"Will and Testament?" John looked confused.

"Yes lad, his last Will and Testament. If he hasn't, and in my experience very few of the settlers here have, I suggest we get it done here and now. I took the liberty of asking the Notary, Mr Wigan here along with me, just in case! You can get on with that while I make my preparations." John looked at William; his eyelids flickered.

"William, it's me John. Can you hear me?" William nodded, almost imperceptibly.

"William, have you made your last Will and Testament?" A slight shake of the head.

"Alright, we need to do that now" William nodded again. John turned to Langley.

"Doctor, is there something you can give him? He is clearly in pain and it will take him all his strength to speak, if he can." Langley searched in his case.

"Yes, we could try him with this. It's an opiate; it might ease the pain for a while." He unstoppered the small blue bottle and pressed it to William's lips. William drank in some of the liquid before the surgeon pulled the bottle away.

"That's enough my friend. That will ease your pain in a few minutes." The surgeon returned to his preparations and Wigan pulled paper, ink and pen from his bag and laid them on the table. John watched as William's face seemed to settle and his breathing, although still shallow, became more steady.

"Can you still here me William?" A nod came again.

"Good. We are going to make your Will. Mr Wigan here is a Notary and he will write it for us bit I'll have to ask you some questions. Can you manage that?"

"Yes" whispered William through his dry lips. Wigan picked up his pen and began writing out the opening

This is to certify that I the undersigned William Gaze of the colony of Swan River Western Australia having been badly wounded by the Natives and my life being at risk do hereby make this my last Will and Testament…

There followed a painful hour in which Wigan asked William questions through John and then John relayed the answers which he dutifully recorded. When asked who should be the Executor of the Will William managed to raise a hand and point to John.

"And what do you wish to be done with all your tools, equipment and belongings Mr Gaze?" asked Wigan. John relayed the question. William's breathing grew more laboured.

"Sell……..all" John nodded and the Notary scratched away.

"And after everything is settled what should be done with any moneys left over?" Again William breathed hard.

"Father……..Emanuel…….home…….Hucclecote". Only the scratching of pen on paper and William's wheezing breath broke the silence.

"There" said Wigan, "it is finished. I will read it back to you and then, if you are in agreement, you can sign it. I will also sign as a witness and you," he turned to one of the soldiers, "you can also witness it. I have written it in a more legal manner than it was dictated to me."

He picked up the document and read in full;

This is to certify that I the undersigned William Gaze of the colony of Swan River Western Australia having been badly wounded by the Natives and my life being at risk do hereby make this my last Will and Testament. I have at the house of John Butler of Fresh Water Bay three boxes of clothes one of the said boxes being of a red colour the other two lead colour, also one tool chest and one packing Till each full of joiners tools also two pit saws and one iron crow bar also one heavy sledge hammer also one set of tools for the purpose of blasting stone also wither four or five sawyers Dogs and one rank Hook. I do hereby also certify that the said John Butler is indebted to me in the sum of forty pounds or thereabouts for building and timber work done at his house. I do hereby authorise and empower John Thomas of Fremantle to sell by public auction all my clothes, tools, chests and all other articles belonging to me and to discharge all expenses attending my funeral also the expenses of the Doctor attending me out of the proceeds of the sale, the overplus together with the said forty pounds due to me from the said John Butler (which I empower him to receive) I request the said John Thomas to remit to Emanuel Gaze of Hucclecote near Gloucester England as witness my mark this fifteenth day of June one thousand eight hundred and thirty two.

After he had finished reading he looked at William. "Is that your wish accurately recorded?" William nodded. "Then you may sign". He held the paper forward and John held the pen in William's hand. "He hasn't the strength to sign his name" protested John.

"Then let him make his mark. We can all witness that he has made the mark"

Mustering a great effort William scratched his mark 'X' on the paper before sinking back into the cot. John handed the paper back.

"I will sign to say that I have witnessed his mark" he did so " and now you" and he offered the pen to the soldier, one John Riley who being unable to write could only scratch his 'X' next to his name. John felt a hand on his and looked down at William. He was trying to speak and he leaned closer.

"Forgot ...more money…..Clark…..Spiers….owe me…..one pound…..thirteen…..shillings"

"Mr Wigan" called John, "there appears to be more". Wigan tutted and drew the document towards him and started writing again. William continued painfully,

"Have had……..eighteen shillings……..eight pence………add to my………money." And with that he lapsed once more into unconsciousness. Wigan completed his sentence and read;

Memo; Since the above signature was made by William Gaze he has declared to me in the presence

of the undersigned witness that Messrs Clark and Spiers Publicans are indebted to him in the sum of one pound thirteen shillings and eight pence out of which amount he has received the sum of eighteen shillings and eight pence the balance of the same account is to be received by the above named John Thomas of Fremantle.

He signed it and asked Riley to do the same again. "Good" said Wigan, "the Will is now complete. I will leave the document in your care Mr Thomas, as you are the named Executor" he coughed "Should things go badly here you know where to find me in Fremantle? Good, then my work here is done and I will bid you goodnight. Mr Thomas, you can expect to receive my bill for drawing up the Will in due course." With that he gathered his materials and with a nod to surgeon Langley he stepped out into the night. Langley stepped up to the now vacant table.

"Right, good timing gentlemen. My preparations are now complete. We will need this table to lay the patient on. Here, you two men, help me move it to the centre of the room so that I can work from both sides." The two soldiers lifted the heavy table and placed it where required.

"Good. Now I will need the patient on here now, on his side please so that I can get to the wounds." Under his directions the inert William was gently lifted and placed on the rough table. Langley laid out his instruments on a cloth; John thought how much they looked like the carpentry tools he had seen William use, the saws, gouges, chisels. The thought was only fleeting for Langley spoke again. "Gentlemen, I will need your assistance to keep him steady. It will not be a very pretty sight I can assure you but you are soldiers and I am sure you are used to a little blood!" unexpectedly he laughed. Standing in his apron with his shirt sleeves rolled tight on his arms he looked more like a jovial country butcher than a surgeon.

"I will start with the cheek wound and then the neck. After that, if he is still alive, we will move to the more serious body wounds." He turned a friendly eye to John. "Are you alright lad?" John nodded. "Good. Then bring that candle closer so that I can see what I am doing."

The two soldiers held William's head steady as John brought the candle nearer. Langley, knife in hand, examined the wound in William's cheek. The spear had pierced the soft fleshy part of the cheek leaving a ragged open wound where it had fallen out. William lay unconscious on the table as Langley probed the wound, deftly cutting away the infected parts and removing some wooden splinters. He said little as he worked, only an occasional "More light here" or "Hold him steady". John marvelled at the speed at which he worked and soon the cheek wound was cleaned and stitched. He looked at John.

"That one was easy my friend. The neck wound will be more complicated." He wiped the bloody instruments on a cloth and passed the back of his hand across his brow. John noticed that he was sweating heavily. He probed the neck wound and William stirred; the two men holding him firm. The spear head was still embedded in the heavily muscled area between the neck and the shoulder. As Langley pointed out to John;

"Fortunately your friend here is a fit and well developed man. The spear has not entered deep enough to hit the spinal cord, although it is firmly lodged."

Cutting into William's flesh the blood began to flow, causing the two soldiers to look at each other, both turning pale, but they did not move from their task. Cutting deeper into the muscle Langley worked his way around the spear head, trying desperately not to tear further flesh or any blood vessels with the barbs. After what seemed like an age he lifted the three inch spear head from the wound and threw it on the floor, where it glistened wetly red in the candlelight. He let out a long sigh and began packing the deep wound with fresh cloth before winding a bandage around William's neck and shoulder to keep it closed. He sat for a moment on a nearby stool, his elbows resting on his knees, head down. His hands were covered in gore and he wiped them on his apron. Shafts of early daylight spread across the darkened windows.

"A drink gentlemen, if I may?"

John filled a beaker from a nearby pitcher and handed it to him. He took it with both hands, oblivious of the blood still there and drank deeply. "Now gentlemen for the difficult part of the work, if you've the stomach for it" and he smiled thinly at the two soldiers again. John took up his position with the candle.

The next spear had been driven through the fleshy part of William's arm and into his ribs, puncturing a lung. It was this that was causing William's breathing problems. On and on the surgeon worked while the others could only look on helplessly, revolted and fascinated at the same time by the cutting and gouging of human flesh. The floor beneath their feet grew slimy with blood and gore and in the candlelight, in his blood stained apron, Langley took on the form of some demonic figure torturing a lost soul in hell. He laboured on as daylight suffused slowly through the gloom of this charnel house. Finally, after hours of painstaking surgery Langley sat heavily on the stool, bloodied spear heads and cloths scattered at his feet.

"There, gentlemen, I can do no more. Only nature will now take its course. He is a relatively young man, fit and bodily tough, and that is good. But now we must wait. The next twenty four hours will tell us if he is to survive or no" and his head sank in exhaustion. John gently washed William's battered body, removing clotted blood from his skin.

William lay as if already dead; only a faint wheezing breath told them he was still alive. Under Langley's direction they carefully lifted him back into his cot. John took up his position next to him as Langley cleaned his instruments and began packing his polished wooden case. By now daylight filled the room; they had worked through the night to save William's life. The two soldiers carried the blood stained table outside and brought in buckets of water to swab the floor. Pulling on his heavy coat Langley turned to John;

"I'll return in twenty four hours. There is little I can do here now. He is in good hands I know. If he wakes wet his lips a little with a damp cloth, otherwise just be patient my friend." John nodded and shook the surgeon's hand, noticing for the first time how small and soft they seemed.

Hours passed and John did not move from William's side. Every so often he placed a damp cloth on William's dry lips and wiped his brow; he was feverish and John hoped the cooling cloth would help. The soldiers came and went, offering him food or to sit with William a while to give John some relief, but John would not break his vigil. Friday became Saturday and still William did not stir. During the day Captain Ellis, the Government Resident in Kelmscott, returned with his detachment of troops. He demanded of John what had happened and John explained through his exhaustion what had happened.

"And what about the leader of this group of natives, the one you saw spear your friend Gaze?"

"He was very distinctive sir" John replied, "very tall and well built for an aboriginal with seemingly more hair and beard than the others."

"Your description Mr Thomas would appear to be that of a well known native by the name of Yagan, or some such name. He and his father, one Midgegooroo the tribal chief, have both been involved in incidents lately around here. It is high time we taught him a lesson, especially now after this!"

He summoned his sergeant to him and ordered a detachment to scour the surrounding countryside for this Yagan, placing a reward for his capture.

"Mr Thomas, I can assure you that this incident will be reported in full to the Colonial Secretary and that action will be taken!"

Very late on Saturday evening William stirred. His eyelids flickered open and his breathing became laboured. John leaned over him.

"William, it's me, John. Can you hear me?"

William's eyes turned towards the sound but did not focus. Words formed on his lips but could not be heard. Tears welled up in John's eyes; he held his hand.

"I'm here friend"

William was aware something was wrong; he could not move. He wanted to but his body did not respond. He had heard a voice, far off, but he could not tell who it was. He wanted to speak but the words would not come. What was happening to him? A pain from deep within racked his body but he could not cry out. Shadows passed across his eyes; shadows from the past. A blurred face appeared momentarily before him and then faded; a woman's face. Sarah? Emily? Mother? He could not tell. Voices came and went inside his head; words, snatches of conversation;

"Look after them tools boy"

"Was I wrong?"

"I want to dance William"

"Don't forget us"

"He's a revolutionary"

"Hey, Billy boy!"

"Come back safe"

And then there was light; so much light, and birdsong and William was lying in the long grass in a Churchdown meadow listening to the church bells. He could smell the new mown hay and he looked up at the brilliant blue sky that faded…..and faded….slowly….to blackness. John felt William's hand slacken in his and a hand on his shoulder.

"He's gone lad, I'm sorry"

John looked up through his tears at surgeon Langley, unaware that he had entered the room. He looked down at William, the unseeing eyes staring at the ceiling. He looked relaxed now, thought John, somehow peaceful. He passed his hand across William's face and closed the eyelids. Then he bent

and gently kissed his friend's forehead.
"God rest you William, wherever you may be."

EPILOGUE

April 2012

Bill stubbed out his cigarette and picked up his coffee as Steve finished the story.

"This is unbelievable!"

"No, it's all fairly well recorded. I've done the research."

"No, I mean you know what happened to Yagan, do you?"

"Yes, the records show he was captured soon after William's death, that he was imprisoned but then escaped and later shot by a young settler. His father Midgegooroo was executed by the British."

"And then?"

"His head was removed, preserved by smoking and then sent back to England as a 'curiosity'. It ended up as an exhibit in the Liverpool Museum for over a hundred years, along with other native body parts from wherever the British colonised."

"Pretty brutal, eh?"

"Yeh, pretty barbaric really. The head was then buried in an unmarked grave with the rest of the exhibits during the 70s somewhere in Everton cemetery. That's an area of Liverpool you know."

"Yes, I know" Bill nodded and smiled as he rolled another cigarette, "and then it was returned to

Australia in 1997." Steve looked up in surprise. "How do you know that?"

"That's what I mean by unbelievable. I mean, what are the odds of us meeting here in this square today? I have an aboriginal friend, Lyndon, who was part of the delegation that went to England to receive Yagan's remains."

"No!"

"Yeh, and did you know that Yagan's head was ceremonially reburied in 2010 in Perth? In a park dedicated to his name, the Yagan Memorial Park?"

"I'd read about it."

"You should go there sometime."

"Well, coincidence upon coincidence, my wife and I are going to Australia this winter. Perth is one of the places we are visiting so now I'll make a point of trying to get to the park as well, it would sort of complete the circle, if you understand my meaning?"

"Yeh, it's a small world isn't it? Look Steve, I've got to go now, my group will be waiting for me outside the cathedral across the square."

"Let me get these" Steve beckoned the young waitress, "la cuenta por favor". She nodded and brought over the bill; Steve placed a handful of Sol on the tray.

"Well, thanks for that Steve. Look, if you ever get as far as Melbourne….."

"That's on our itinerary as well, we're staying with friends there."

"Good, then here's my email address" and both men scribbled down their contact details and exchanged them. "Keep in touch and if you ever get that far then maybe we'll meet up if I'm around. Maybe we can get Lyndon along as well."

"I'd like that. It would be good."

"Then thanks again for the coffee."

"My pleasure."

"And keep in touch, yeh?"

"I will."

Emerging out of the café into the warm sun the two men shook hands again and went their separate ways, both musing over how the life of one man so long ago had brought them together on that day in one of life's strange coincidences

HISTORICAL NOTES

THE GAZE FAMILY

Churchdown parish records show that William Gaze was baptised on the 10th January 1801, son of Emanuel and Mary Gaze. The Gazes were an extended family of wheelwrights and carpenters and plied their trade in Churchdown near Gloucester and the surrounding villages. Little is known of William's early life but it is recorded in the Parish Overseers records that the Gaze family was in receipt of Parish Relief during his formative years. William became indentured to Thomas Peel and travelled to the Swan River Colony on board the ship the Gilmore, arriving in December 1829. The State Library of Western Australia holds original records concerning the court case against Peel; the circumstances of William's death; his Will and other correspondence relating. The Will was granted probate on the 14th August 1832, the first probate to be granted in the Colony, and was recorded as Number 1 Page 1. Whether his father ever received the balance of his Estate is never recorded but the family must have been informed of William's death because it is recorded on the Gaze family memorial headstone in the churchyard of St Bartholomew's Churchdown;

WILLIAM GAZE
their eldest son
killed by the natives
on Swan River Island
June 17th 1832

George Gaze, William's cousin, went on to marry Elizabeth Hiccups and they lived in Upton St Leonard, Gloucester. They produced a daughter Mary and subsequently my lineage. George is my x3 Great Grandfather.

THOMAS PEEL

After the court case in which William was freed of his indentures Peel took up the offer of a land grant and sailed with his son south to the Murray River area, setting up home in the settlement of Mandurah. He proved an incompetent and inefficient farmer and many of his settlers left his land, leaving him almost alone. His wife and other children joined him from England for a short while but then returned, leaving Peel and his son in Mandurah. He ran up large debts and had to begin to sell off his land to cover these. He died in relative poverty in 1865 in Mandurah and is buried there.

The township of Clarence was abandoned by the end of 1830 and is now the site of an archaeological dig.

SOLOMON LEVEY

Levey approached the Government in 1830 to enquire as to what had happened to Peel and his plans for the Swan River Colony. He was refused any information as the Colonial Office had no knowledge of his involvement in the scheme. He died in 1833, having invested and lost much of his capital in Peel's failed venture.

JAMES STIRLING

In 1838 Captain James Stirling relinquished his post of Lieutenant Governor of the Colony and resumed his naval career. His last command was as Commander in Chief, China and East India Station in 1854. By this time he had risen to the rank of Admiral. He died at home in England in 1865.

JOHN THOMAS

After the murder of William John decided to return to Fremantle and continue working on the sea. In 1846 he was in a position to have built a schooner for himself and became captain of his own ship. He traded around the coasts of Australia and then further afield to Mauritius, Singapore and the Cape. In 1876 he retired from the sea and joined his wife on their land he had purchased in Pinjarra, where he died a well respected member of the community.

YAGAN

The process of lobbying and the repatriation of Yagan's head took thirteen years to complete. Lead by Ken Colbung, a delegation of aboriginal leaders formerly received the head from the British Government in 1997. In 2010 the head was buried with due ceremony in the new Yagan Memorial Park at Belhus, east of Perth in the Upper Swan Valley; a project funded by the Western Australia State Government. The Park depicts traditional Nyoongar life pre colonisation and early contact with the new settlers up until the death of Yagan in 1833. Yagan has been described as 'a hero who stood up for land rights at a time when the fledgling Swan River Colony was the western frontier'.

THE SWAN RIVER COLONY

The Colony never fully developed as a business venture as had been planned. Although the climate was generally acceptable to European settlers the land was not as productive as had been thought. By 1850, only two decades after its founding, the population of the entire colony stood at only around 5500 people, two thirds of which "would quit the colony tomorrow", according to the Governor Charles Fitzgerald. In 1846 a request was sent to the British Government, requesting that the Swan River Colony, now known as Western Australia, be made a convict settlement area. Accordingly in 1850 the first ship load of convicts arrived in Fremantle, the last area of Australia to accept convicts. The subsequent prosperity of the area was built upon convict labour.

NYOONGAR WORDS

The Nyoongar were the indigenous Australian
people who lived in the Swan River area at the time
of colonisation. Traditionally they made a living
from hunting and trapping game. The following
Nyoongar words are used throughout this novel as
given in the word list on the website
www.wheatbeltnrm.org.au

Kitj	spear
Waana	digging stick
Karl	fire
Mirlen	flowering stem with honey like gum
Bardi	witchitte grub
Kep	water
Wanju	welcome
Kutj	skin bag (usually kangaroo)
Dhatj	food
Ngardanginy	hunting
Merrany barang	fruit gathering
Djurlap	loincloth
Moort	family
Yonga	kangaroo
Kaya	greeting or approval
Yanamarru nhurra	come here

Acknowledgements

The author would like to thank the following people
and organisations for their help in supplying
information for this book;

The Gloucester Archives; Ivor Smith; Colleen
Fancote and members of the Kelmscott Local
History Group; The Pioneer Settler Association of
Western Australia; The State Library of Western
Australia (the Battye Collection); Lyndon Ormond-
Parker; Marcia Langton of the University of
Melbourne; Shane Burke of Notre Dame University
Fremantle; Bill Snoek

Articles on the life of William Gaze have been previously
published by the author in the following magazines;

Family History Monthly
UK   February 2012

Australian Family Tree Connections
Australia   October 2012

Proof

Made in the USA
Charleston, SC
13 January 2013